SIGNS OF THE TIMES:
The Great Persecution

JOE IRIZARRY

Signs of the Times: The Great Persecution
Copyright © 2022 by Joe Irizarry

All rights reserved. No part of this publication may be reproduced, distributed, or transmitted in any form or by any means, including photocopying, recording, or other electronic or mechanical methods, without the prior written permission of the publisher or author, except in the case of brief quotations embodied in critical reviews and certain other noncommercial uses permitted by copyright law.

ISBN: (Paperback) 978-1-63945-532-4
       (Hardcover) 978-1-63945-533-1
       (eBook)   978-1-63945-534-8

The views expressed in this book are solely those of the author and do not necessarily reflect the views of the publisher, and the publisher hereby disclaims any responsibility for them.

Writers' Branding
1-800-608-6550
www.writersbranding.com
orders@writersbranding.com

DEDICATION

This book is dedicated to the countless Christians who have given their lives for Jesus and those who have suffered because of their faith in Him.

- J.I.

CONTENTS

PREFACE vii

CHAPTER 1 - CHINA 1
CHAPTER 2 - EGYPT 13
CHAPTER 3 - SAUDI ARABIA 23
CHAPTER 4 - SUDAN 35
CHAPTER 5 - SYRIA 47
CHAPTER 6 - IRAQ 59
CHAPTER 7 - INDIA 69
CHAPTER 8 - NIGERIA. 81
CHAPTER 9 - IRAN 93
CHAPTER 10 - PAKISTAN 105
CHAPTER 11 - LIBYA 115
CHAPTER 12 - SOMALIA. 125
CHAPTER 13 - NORTH KOREA 135
CHAPTER 14 - AFGHANISTAN. 145

Epilogue 155

PREFACE

"Then you will be delivered to persecution and death, and you will be hated by all nations because of me." Matthew 24:9

What is the definition of persecution? Persecutory behavior is defined as the act of harassing or oppressing a person or a group of people because of their race, ethnicity, political or religious convictions. In addition, persecution includes animosity, mistreatment, and may even include murder, of those who are targeted.

Open Doors, an international organization that campaigns on behalf of oppressed or persecuted Christians, published its annual World Watch List in January 2022. The World Alliance List assesses the fifty nations in which Christians are subject to the most serious types of persecution.

Several factors can contribute to the persecution of Christians, including: the connection between religion and ethnic or cultural identity at times. For example, in power-hungry countries that consider Christianity a threat, of which their governments regard Jesus as a competitor, and the people who follow him as a danger to their ability to maintain control over their citizens. Some countries attach great importance to their majority religion and any other faith is seen as something that must be uprooted and forcibly restricted by the majority religion.

Christianity is persecuted in several nations, especially those ruled by authoritarian governments. Authoritarian regimes, such as North Korea and China, attempt to maintain strict control over all religious beliefs and expressions as part of a global plan to strictly regulate all elements of politics and daily life in their respective countries. These governments regard some religious organizations as enemies of the state because they adhere to religious ideas, which are incompatible with the authorities' desire for total loyalty.

In some places, there is considerable hatred towards non-Orthodox and minority religious organizations, which are perceived as alien or non-native to the local culture. For example; in Niger, where more than 98% of the population is Muslim, animosity comes mainly from the general public and not from the authorities. Hindu nationalists in India often claim that to be Indian is to be Hindu. Therefore, non-Hindus (religious minorities such as Christians and Muslims) are subject to persecution. In these areas, to be a Christian is to affirm an identity different from that affirmed by the prevailing culture, and that identity is often fiercely rejected.

In various parts of the world there are radicalized extremist groups that wage war on all those who do not adhere to their particular interpretation of religious teachings. Islamic extremist organizations such as Boko Haram, the Taliban or ISIS, for example, harass villages and churches in places in the Middle East and

Nigeria and regularly murder people they consider "infidels" (often in coordinated attacks). They have been known to rape and kidnap women and destroy homes and churches. Their main target is Christians, because of their hostility towards people of other religions. In some cases, its victims are co-religionists of the Muslim religion (for example, Boko Haram is known to attack other Muslims in Nigeria).

Religious freedom, like all other freedoms of thought and expression, is inherent in America. American values have helped define who we are as individuals and have served as the basis for our contributions to the societies we have influenced. Although the United States is a free society, many people around the world currently live under regimes that impede or restrict their right to practice religion freely. Christians in these areas are subjected to severe suffering and are denied the fundamental freedoms to which all human beings should be entitled.

There are many areas in the world where official laws have been enacted that strictly limit or even prevent Christians from freely expressing their faith or proselytizing, all under the pretext of serving the interests of a dominant religion.

Suppose you live in a Muslim-majority country, such as the Maldives or Saudi Arabia. In that case, it is almost unheard of to attempt to worship Jesus, especially outside of openly approved (and limited) scenarios. Laws in areas like Pakistan are dictated by Islamic law, implying that a Christian accused of "blasphemy" could be sentenced to death. Christians in Iran are only allowed to attend services in churches that do not speak Persian, the language of the Iranian people at large. In addition, there are strict rules on conversion from Islam for certain ethnic groups, in places like Malaysia.

In the first book in this series, **Signs of the Times in 2020**; the persecution was dealt with in one chapter, but requires further examination because of the current state of the world.

Although Christian persecution takes various forms, it is characterized as any hostility encountered due to affiliation with Jesus Christ. Followers of Christianity are targeted for persecution for their religion in all parts of the world: they are attacked at work and school, discriminated against, at risk of being sexually assaulted, tortured, detained and much more.

The prophets of the Bible predicted the end-time persecution, and this is what we will focus on. We will focus on the current oppression that Christians face, so that prophecy becomes a reality before our eyes. Much of the media around the world has turned a blind eye to these current developments. It is claimed that many will be amazed at the news of the current persecution facing the church around the world. In fact, we are in the biblical end time that the prophets wrote about.

This book will expose fourteen countries where Christians are persecuted for their faith. Countries are classified according to the severity of Christian persecution and are calculated by analyzing the level of violent persecution in five spheres of life (private, family, community, national and ecclesiastical) plus the pressure experienced.

Hebreos 11:35-40 (NVI)

"The women received their dead, resurrected. Others were tortured, refusing to be released to obtain an even better resurrection. Some faced ridicule and whipping, and even chains and imprisonment. They died stoned, cut in two, killed by the sword. They went back and forth in sheep and goat skins, destitute, persecuted and mistreated: the world was not worthy of them. They roamed deserts and mountains, living in caves and holes in the earth. All of them were praised for their faith, but none of them received what was promised, since God had planned something better for us, so that only together with us would they be perfected."

We see many examples of persecution throughout the Bible, showing that hardship is nothing new for God's children. There are numerous accounts of people who were tortured and executed in the book of Hebrews, chapter 11, for the sake of the gospel. Some were thrown into a fiery furnace, while others were thrown into the lions. Some were killed by the sword, while others were stoned to death by a mob. They died with the peace of knowing that they had resisted because of their faith.

And the clock keeps ticking, ticking, ticking...

China

CHAPTER 1

CHINA

"Do not be afraid of what you are going to suffer. I tell you that the devil will put some of you in jail to prove you, and that you will suffer persecution for ten days. Be faithful unto death, and I will give you life as a crown of overcomers." Revelation 2:10

*****

In today's world, we hear almost daily reports through Chinese Communist Party watchdog groups threatening churches, pastors, or groups of believers. Unfortunately, the world's mainstream media has been silent about the religious persecutions and crimes against humanity perpetrated in China, including internment camps for people of faith.

On December 10, 2018, the U.S. State Department listed China among the *"Countries of Special Concern"* for serious violations of religious rights. "Flagrant violations" include "torture, degrading treatment or punishment, prolonged detention without charge, kidnapping or clandestine detention," as well as "other flagrant violations of the right to life, liberty, or security of persons," according to the State Department's Bureau of Democracy, Human Rights, and Labor. China ranked 27th in 2019, 23rd in 2020 and 17th in 2021 on the *Open Door World Watch* List of the fifty countries where being a Christian is most difficult. According to data compiled by Open Doors USA, the persecution of Christians has increased considerably in the previous three years and the growing trend is expected to continue for the foreseeable future.

Digital surveillance in churches.

China's churches are being monitored more closely than at any time since Mao's Cultural Revolution (1966-1976). In 1976, when Chairman Mao Zedong passed away, he left a legacy of millions of corpses sacrificed on the altar of socialism, many of whom were Christians. According to the authoritative *"Black Book of Communism,"* an estimated 65 million Chinese perished due to Mao Zedong's repeated and relentless efforts to establish a new "socialist" China. He wiped out anyone who stood in his way, whether through execution, imprisonment, or forced starvation, among other methods.

According to *Release International*, a Christian advocacy organization that helps persecuted Christians, China has been stepping up its attack on the Chinese Church under the pretext of Covid-19 restrictions. On January 22, 2021, *Release International* issued a warning that persecution of Christians is likely to intensify in the coming year as a result of growing intolerance in Hong Kong, including increased digital surveillance in churches.

Because the country's half a trillion digital surveillance cameras are linked to the social security system, officials have the authority to withdraw welfare or pension payments from those who are ambiguously considered "criminals."

Bob Fu, a Chinese-American pastor and pro-democracy activist who is currently living in exile in the United States and a contributor to *Release International*, said:

"Digital authoritarianism is becoming a major concern. The Chinese Communist Party installed facial recognition cameras in hundreds of millions of locations across the country. They watch every corner, and they do it from the four walls of religious structures and even from pulpits."

Punished Christians.

According to the *World Christian Movement* (a non-denominational parachurch ministry that collaborates with churches around the world), restrictions, pressure, warnings, and even surprise raids on churches are part of the rapidly expanding Chinese church Christian experience In 2021. Chinese Christians are also experiencing an increase in persecution in their workplaces. For example, Christians who openly follow Jesus and share his faith can be singled out to be treated harshly. It has been reported that if Christians refuse to substitute Christian imagery, such as crosses, for images of President Xi Jinping, Communist Party officials in Shanxi and other provinces, such as Henan and Jiangxi, have threatened to withhold social benefits, including pensions. As reported at the time, in May 2020 crosses and icons of Jesus were removed from the home of a church minister, and replaced by a photograph of Mao Zedong.

As one anonymous preacher put it, *"the government is trying to eliminate our belief and wants to become God... Since the new religious regulations were enforced more strongly in 2018, churches have also experienced increased pressure and reduced visibility."* (The preacher is not named for security reasons)

The government actively persecutes unregistered house churches to "invite" them to apply for registration; otherwise, they are considered illegal and can be raided by law enforcement.

The Chinese Communist Party has long viewed autonomous religious activity as a challenge to its regulation. Although the party does not intend to abolish religion, it challenges it and seeks the loyalty and dedication of religious followers. Also, if you can't replace it, at least try to co-opt it.

The persecution of believers has intensified under Xi Jinping's Sinicization Program, which began in 2014. With the Chinese government in complete control of the judicial system, authorities routinely accuse pastors of subversion, as religion is seen as a threat to the Chinese Communist Party and the country's overall stability. These pastors are not entitled to legal representation. If someone is brave enough to be your advocate, the pastor may be beaten before meeting. Your lawyer may also be beaten.

The program also strives to secularize the religion in an attempt to ensure that it promotes the goals of the Chinese Communist Party. Sinicization has traditionally been carried out through the creation of state-sanctioned religious institutions that moderate and change the way people of all faiths practice their religion.

Pastor Wang Yi

As a result of increased religious persecution in China, Pastor Wang Yi, leader of one of the country's largest unregistered churches, has been sentenced to nine years in prison on charges of subversion of government authority and illegal business operations.

When law enforcement raided different locations in the Chengdu (Sichuan) area on December 9, 2018, they arrested Pastor Wang, founder of the Early Rain Covenant Church, along with more than 100 members of it. Before they were released, most of the members had been interrogated and tortured into making false accusations against Pastor Wang. More than 500 people participated in the "illegal" Church.

The subversion charges the state brought against Pastor Wang of Early Rain called for a sentence of between five and fifteen years in extreme circumstances for "inciting subversion of state authority" and "illegal business operations." The trial, which took place on December 26, 2019, was attended only by lawyers, the judge and Pastor Wang. A police cordon surrounded the room and no family members, friends, church members or the press were allowed to enter. The

Chengdu Intermediate People's Court announced his punishment in a secret judicial process, after more than a year of imprisonment in the city. Finally, Wang Yi, pastor of the Early Rain Covenant Church in Chengdu, China, was sentenced to nine years in prison on Monday, December 30, 2019. Over the next three years, Wang will also be denied political rights and his assets, estimated to be worth about 50,000 yuan (US$7,200), will be confiscated.

Before becoming a pastor, Pastor Wang was a human rights activist and constitutional scholar. When Pastor Wang and Jiang Rong's son, Shu Ya, then eleven, was arrested, he was left in the care of Pastor Wang's mother, Chen Yaxue, who subsequently became his legal guardian.

Every time Shu Ya and his grandmother went out, they were subject to police surveillance and were followed by the agents.

The couple reunited after Shu Ya's release, but are reportedly under house arrest in a secret location and closely monitored by authorities.

Assault on Shanghai Church.

According to the China Aid Association (CAA), police stormed the Wheat Church in Shanghai on December 1, 2020. When the agents broke into the Church, it was in the middle of a worship session. They alleged that the participants were engaged in religious activities in an illegal location. They stopped the preaching of the Church and took all its faithful out of the interior of the building. Some 200 Christians stood firm in front of the church and refused to flee. They sang and worshiped standing in the cold.

According to Chinese religious laws, religious activities are only allowed in designated places. Following that incident, the authorities continued with heavy surveillance in known worship areas.

Since Xi Jinping became China's president in 2013, the Chinese Communist Party has taken increasingly stringent measures against Christianity and other religions it sees as a threat to the party's authority. New religious norms adopted in 2017 significantly increase the number of government entities that can apply limitations to religious practice. Under these new religious directives, house churches have been forced to dissolve if they do not register under the new religious directives, adding that they are subject to surveillance, sermon tracking and other mass measures. The current persecution of the Chinese Church by the Communist Party has been the subject of Open Doors reports in recent years.

The Christian threat.

Following the signing of China's Agreement with the Vatican, the current limitations on Christian customs began to harden further in 2018. Since then, many churches have been closed, largely unofficial organizations and some recognized by the government. There have been between 5,000 and 10,000 arrests of Christian worshippers, several famous Protestant clerics have been sentenced to long prison terms, and about two-thirds of the country's Protestants have turned to underground churches in an attempt to avoid police harassment.

Government authorities have been responsible for collecting more information on the faithful and contributing to discrimination in employment, especially in government positions. All persons under the age of 18 have been prohibited from participating in any form of religious education, which was already the case in theory but had not been strictly enforced in practice until recently. Based on current expectations, religious leaders are expected to spend more time personally praising the Chinese Communist Party and Chinese President Xi Jinping than their congregations. Images of Jesus have already been replaced by images of Xi in various places of worship.

Of course, the attack on Christian practice in China is neither new nor unprecedented. The Chinese Communist Party has traditionally imposed restrictions on believers, and the relationship between Chinese imperial powers and religion was often strained. Emperor Wuzong of the Tang Dynasty, who reigned from 827 to 840, intended to purify China of foreign influences. Their goal was Buddhism, which was a foreign Indian religion, and Nestorian Christianity and Manichaeism were also considered foreign religions. Christianity and the missionaries who accompanied it were intimately linked to the Western imperial powers that tore apart the Chinese empire during what Chinese historians call the "Age of Humiliation." China's current obsession with "foreign" religions has its roots in the Qing dynasty of the nineteenth century. China's ruling elite's distrust of foreign religion was only reinforced by the Taiping Rebellion, led by an eccentric Chinese Christian leader who preached his localized interpretation of the faith and was accompanied by Islamist uprisings across the country.

Christianity, on the other hand, may be the most widespread of all the numerous identities imaginable. In China, statistics are hard to come by, but there can be as many as 100 million believers, which is significantly more than the 90 million members of the Chinese Communist Party. Some estimates predict as many as 250 million Christians in China by 2030, which is slightly optimistic. All this makes the faith, however divergent and disunited Christian belief, inherently dangerous for the Communist Party of China. Chinese leaders have also paid close attention to the disintegration of the Soviet Union. They are well aware of the importance of the Catholic and Protestant faith in ending communism in Eastern Europe during the Cold War.

Chinese internment camps.

The Xinjiang internment camps, formally known as Xinjiang Vocational Education and Training Centers by the Chinese government, are detention centers run by the Xinjiang Uygur Autonomous Region and the provincial committee of the Chinese Communist Party. Human Rights Watch has reported that the facilities have been used to indoctrinate Uighurs and other Muslims since 2017 as part of China's "people's war on terror," a strategyfirst proclaimed in 2014.

Human rights groups and governments around the world have condemned the camps for alleged human rights violations, including ill-treatment, rape and torture, with some claiming genocide has occurred. Some nations have expressed support for Chinese leaders by flatly rejecting accusations of genocide and explaining the presenceof internment camps.

According to the Chinese government, Christians, Muslim Uighurs, and Falun Gong practitioners are treated equally in China. The persecution of religious minorities has reached new heights under Chinese President Xi Jinping and the Chinese Communist Party, with statistics exceeding those observed duringMao Zedong's Cultural Revolution.

Lately, the Chinese Communist Party has imprisoned the vast majority of the Uighur Muslim population in the westernmost part of Xinjiang to remain in prison: Beijing appears to have built 260 extra-high-security detention centers to house them, according to satellite images.

In 2017, the Chinese Communist Party planned and interned Muslim Uighurs in China's political re-education centers.

Early estimates of a few hundred thousand people interned in the camps were quickly updated to reflect the exact picture: camps housing approximately 1.8 million Uighurs. Fields are sometimes (or perhaps always) associated with factories; this makes the prisoners alegal slave for the state.

The lucky few who were eventually released told stories of how they heard the screams of their neighbors being tortured at the end of the hallway. Torture included obstructive sterilizationand other atrocities.

Beijing maintains that there are no human rights violations in Xinjiang. Chinese officials ended up characterizing the detention camps as "vocational training and re-education programs" aimed at alleviating poverty and preventing terrorism problems, following initial refusals.

The foundations and founding principles of the Chinese Communist Party are based on lies. One of the lies is the ridiculous claim that religious believers are only punished when they break the law, which is totally false. The U.S. Commission on International Religious Freedom (USCIRF) and other groups have documented several incidents of Christians, Uighurs, Tibetans, and Falun Gong practitioners who have been imprisoned solely for practicing their beliefs.

And the clock keeps ticking, ticking, ticking...

Egypt

CHAPTER 2

EGYPT

"In fact, everyone who wants to live a godly life in Christ Jesus will be persecuted."
2 Timothy 3:12

Modern Egypt is well known for being a Muslim country. What is less well known is that Egypt has also been home to Coptic Christians, commonly known as Copts. Coptic Christians are a group of people who can trace their ethnic heritage back to the days of the ancient Egyptians and their Christian lineage to the times of the apostle Mark. They are the largest and oldest ethnoreligious minority in the country, having lived in it for thousands of years. As their roots are claimed to date back to the time of Jesus, they are considered one of the oldest Christian groups on the planet.

For most of the past 2000 years, the Coptic Orthodox Church of Egypt has been subject to tremendous persecution. The persecution, which began during Roman authority in the first century, increased in intensity following the Arab invasion of the region in 640 AD.

Egypt's Coptic Christians have been subjected to oppression and brutality on numerous occasions throughout history. Those belonging to the Orthodox Christian minority thought that the Arab Spring and the coming to power of Abdel Fattah Al-Sisi on June 8, 2014, would bring with it more civil and religious liberties. After being persecuted by Islamists and other extremists, that dream was once again dashed.

Today, the majority of Egypt's Coptic Christians, estimated at between 6 and 11 million people, live mainly in the provincial capitals of Asyut and Minya in Upper Egypt and in the capital, Cairo. Although Copts have been an integral part of Egyptian society for generations, they have been subject to widespread prejudice and persecution, especially after the Arab Spring of 2011.

"Dhimmis" is a pejorative term used to refer to Christians by the new Arab rulers, who considered them polytheistic and therefore deserving of protected status (protected subjects), thus relegating them to the status of second-class citizens. Discriminatory laws and decrees reinforce their status as second-class citizens, requiring many Copts to pay additional taxes to which Muslims are not subject.

Religious persecution.

The persecution of Christians in Egypt is mainly concentrated at the community level. In Upper Egypt, where Salafist groups (Al-Qaeda, ISIS, Boko Haram and Al-Shabaab) significantly influence rural populations due to high levels of illiteracy and poverty, incidents occur more frequently. These incidents can range from the approach of Christian ladies as they walk down the street, the theft of Christian girls, their forced conversion and sale to Muslim men, and Christian communities being forced to leave their homes by extreme mobs.

Al-Azhar University, one of the world's most illustrious Islamic institutions, occupies an important position in Egyptian society, and its name even appears in the country's national anthem. According to the university's Grand Imam, Ahmed el-Tayyeb, Muslim converts to Christianity have been categorically denied a place in Islam. Christians of Muslim origin have enormous difficulties in living their religious convictions, as they are under intense pressure from their families to return to their religion of origin.

The Egyptian authorities have openly expressed their support for the Christian community. However, the lack of serious law enforcement and the unwillingness of local authorities to protect Christians have made them vulnerable to a wide range of attacks, especially in Upper Egypt, where the Christian population is concentrated. Church leaders and other Christians cannot denounce these activities because of the authoritarian nature of government administration.

In addition, Christian churches and non-governmental organizations (NGOs) are restricted in the construction of new churches, the maintenance of church buildings or the provision of social services, which contrasts with the treatment of mosques and Islamic organizations. Christians of various faiths have difficulty finding new places of community worship. The limitations of the state, the animosity of the community and the violence of the mafias contribute to the problems faced by the community.

The ability of Christians to create and maintain ecclesiastical buildings remains restricted by state organizations. Even when they have been granted permission to rebuild or build new churches, local Muslims often oppose their attempts to carry out those plans. Copts have been forced to make concessions, such as the construction of churches without bells or towers, which is the usual consequence of reconciliation procedures sponsored by local authorities. Often, the commitments that Christians endure fail to bring justice to the victims of sectarian violence.

In addition, in August 2016, a new rule on ecclesiastical buildings was approved that transfers the authority to build and reform churches outside the security services and into the hands of provincial governors. According to many human rights defenders, this is a "prejudiced and sectarian" law, as it shows that the state prefers one faith over another.

Disagreements and tensions over church buildings have played an important role in initiating sectarian violence, especially severe in the Minya governorate of Upper Egypt. The Egyptian authorities have consistently failed to protect the rights of their Christian citizens. In the absence of formal judicial investigations, local disputes are often resolved through informal "reconciliation" sessions that do not contribute to discouraging intolerance and impunity in the country's Christian communities.

Religious persecution remains a source of constant concern for Egypt's Christians. To prevent the gains made during Al-Sisi's rule from unraveling in the future, a cultural transformation is needed that ensures equal citizenship for all religious communities, while ending religious persecution.

Because of the deep roots of religious persecution, the Coptic community has seen significant advances in its status throughout its history, only for them to be swept away by new political forces. In various parts of the Middle East, Christians are targeted for murder. Although persecution is widespread, it is especially severe in Syria, Iraq and Egypt, to name a few countries. Recently, Egypt's Coptic Christians have been attacked by both Islamists and non-jihadist Egyptians.

The Copts of Egypt constitute approximately 10% of the Egyptian population. However, they have been targeted by Islamist organizations and other Egyptians in recent decades, as sectarianism became present throughout the country and terrorism spread from Syria's conflict zone, according to National Review. ISIS has claimed responsibility for several church bombings, including the two 2017 Palm Sunday attacks that claimed the lives of 45 souls and injured more than 100.

At least seven Coptic Christians were killed and 18 injured when terrorists ambushed a bus taking them to the monastery of Anba Samuel the Confessor in Minya, Upper Egypt, in November 2018. They were on their way to visit the monastery. Less than 18 months later, masked shooters opened fire on a convoy of Coptic Christians, killing 28 and wounding 23 in the same area.

These violent attacks are part of a broader and longer pattern of discrimination and religious persecution suffered by Egypt's Coptic population. Persecution is not a phrase to be taken lightly; according to the Rome Statute of the International Criminal Court, persecution is defined as "the deliberate and serious denial of fundamental rights in violation of international law on the basis of the identification of a group or collectivity".

In recent years, it seems that violence has not decreased. There have reportedly been more attacks on the Coptic Christian minority. Three houses of Coptic Christians were set on fire and demolished in response to a false accusation that one of the residents of a Coptic Christian residence had insulted Islam on Facebook. The alleged perpetrator of the message was arrested for alleged violation of blasphemy laws, but the individuals who set fire to the houses were not arrested or imprisoned in any way.

Such scenes occur all too often in Egypt, and they must be dealt with. In many cases, it is both extremist jihadist organizations that perpetrate violence against Christians and ordinary Egyptians carry out this brutality. In general, many Egyptians regard Christians as heretics who commit blasphemy against Islam.

In Egypt and elsewhere, the world community has mainly overlooked anti-Christian violence, which is a tragedy. In general, they remain deafeningly mute on the subject of Christian persecution. On the other hand, it is reasonable to believe that if Christians persecuted Muslims on a large scale, the story would be front-page news around the world.

As Christians, we must take a stand and declare that the oppression of any group based on their religious beliefs, regardless of their ethnicity or geographical location, is simply unacceptable.

In addition, ISIS has frequently vowed to "go after Egypt's Christians as punishment" for its support for President Al-Sisi in recent years. The terrorist group has horrified the entire world by carrying out a series of horrific attacks on Christians, whom they refer to as their "favorite prey."

JOE IRIZARRY

The US Secretary of State emphasizes human rights in Egypt.

Egyptian President Al-Sisi and U.S. Secretary of State Antony J. Blinken met in Cairo, Egypt, on May 26, 2021. They underlined the importance of human rights when religious freedom in the nation is threatened. Both Egypt and the United States agreed to hold a productive debate on the promotion and protection of human rights for all Egyptians, as part of their efforts to strengthen their bilateral partnership. However, given Egypt's troubled history. However, given Egypt's troubled human rights and religious freedom history, it is not clear that Secretary Blinken's suggestions will be a significant step forward.

While Secretary Blinken's meeting with President al-Sisi offers a glimmer of optimism for the future of human rights in the nation, the country's inability to safeguard religious minorities shows that much more needs to be done. Egypt has done good diplomatic work to promote peace in the area, as evidenced by its recent mediation in a truce between Israel and Gaza. However, the United States should not turn a blind eye to the plight of Egyptian minorities to appease the Egyptian government.

Egypt's position on the World Watch List has remained consistent in the 20th worst place to be a Christian since 2022, despite a modest rise in overall anti-Christian sentiment over the previous year. Although there has been less recent violence against

Christians in Egypt, there has been more significant opposition in the community.

And the clock keeps ticking, ticking, ticking...

Saudi Arabia

CHAPTER 3

SAUDI ARABIA

"I saw thrones on which sat those who had received authority to judge. And I saw the souls of those who had been beheaded for their testimony about Jesus and for the word of God. They had not worshiped the beast or its image and had not received its mark on the forehead or hand. They came back to life and reigned with Christ for a thousand years." Revelation 20:4

*****

According to the Constitution of Saudi Arabia, the establishment of any non-Muslim public place of worship is strictly prohibited, as Saudi Arabia does not protect freedom of religion. The government gives preference to Sunni Islam over all other Islamic sects. Even dissident clerics and members of Saudi Arabia's Shiite Islamic community (the largest religious minority) continue to be repressed and discriminated against by the state. According to an official Saudi government text, the law prohibits "any attempt to cast doubt on the foundations of Islam," publications that "contradict the provisions of Islamic law," other acts such as non-Islamic public devotion, including the public display of non-Islamic symbols, the conversion of a Muslim to another faith, and the proselytizing of non-Muslims. Moreover, under a 2014 law, atheism in any of its forms or questioning the foundations of the Islamic religion, on which Saudi Arabia is based, is prohibited under Article 1 of the "terrorist" status. Those who disagree with the state are often persecuted and imprisoned, and those individuals who convert from Islam to a different religion may be sentenced to the death penalty. The law was introduced by royal decree and there was no judicial oversight or scrutiny.

Based on these egregious violations of religious freedom, the U.S. Commission on International Religious Freedom (USCIRF) recommends that Saudi Arabia be recognized as a "country of special concern" or CPC under the International Religious Freedom Act of 2015 (IRFA). Although the United States has designated Saudi Arabia as a CPC on multiple occasions since 2004, the most recent designation was in July 2014; an indefinite waiver prohibiting the United States from taking other legally binding measures as a result of designation as a CPC has been in effect since 2006. Usually, in cases where the Secretary of State appoints a CPC, Congress is notified of the designation. When non-economic political options (designed to prevent particularly serious violations of religious freedom) have been reasonably exhausted, an economic measure may be imposed.

Although Saudi Arabia is an Islamic state, it has between eight and ten million foreign employees of various religions, among whom there are at least one or two million non-Muslims. While the Saudi government has taken some steps to address legitimate concern about religious extremism and advocacy of violence in sermons and educational materials, other government actions appear to contradict progress by continuing to restrict peaceful religious practices and expression in suppressing the religious views and practices of Saudi and non-Saudi Muslims that do not conform to official positions. In addition, the government has not formalized the protection of the private religious practices of non-Muslim expatriate employees in the nation, contributing to the sense of unrest. Although Saudi Arabia remains the only country banning public expression of any religion other than Islam, there has been some progress on religious freedom. Despite recent improvements in policies and practices related to freedom of religion or belief, the Saudi government restricts most forms of free worship incompatible with its particular interpretation of Sunni Islam.

The death of former King Abdullah bin Abdulaziz Al Saud took place on 23 January 2015. He was replaced by his half-brother, then Crown Prince Salman bin Abdulaziz al Saud, who ascended the throne immediately. Many of his predecessor's initiatives have been continued by King Salman, including implementing a Saudi foreign policy dedicated to the teachings of Islam and safeguarding the country's legal Sharia system. In addition, "anyone who questions, directly or indirectly, the faith or justice of the king or crown prince is subject to criminal prosecution," according to the law.

Almost non-existent Christians.

In Saudi Arabia, any religious manifestation other than Islam is strictly prohibited, as the law is based on the Wahhabi interpretation of Islam.

Christians residing in Saudi Arabia face significant resistance to their faith, whether Saudi or foreign. For example, Saudi citizens who are Christians must practice their faith in secret, risking jail and possible execution if they practice it in public. Foreign workers who are Christians in Saudi Arabia are also not allowed to express their religious beliefs in public.

The nation opened its doors to international tourists for the first time in September 2021. Although the rules for tourists in relation to Bibles and other Christian items are undeniably repressive, recently the rules have been slightly relaxed, as visitors are now allowed to carry a cross or a Bible for personal use. It wasn't like that before. Previously, visitors were confiscated crosses or Bibles, and expelled from the country if they were found in possession of material with religious motives.

Although Saudi Arabia is making progress on tolerance, all visitors entering the country should be warned that displaying a Bible in public or bringing more than one Bible tothe country can result in prison sentences. If any other religiously motivated material is discovered, the individual may be expelled from the country or face additional punishment.

The few Saudi Christians of Muslim descent are under immense pressure, especially from their families, to convert. One of the most serious crimes a Muslim can commit is to abandon Islam. Men can be subjected to physical and mental abuse, as well as public humiliation. Material incentives are offered to persuade individuals to recant, but rejecting them can lead to death. For their part, women can be subjected to various penalties, such as forced marriage, divorce, sexual assault and house arrest. The servile status of women in Saudi society may add additional difficulties to flight. No wonder many Christians, whether men or women, want to keep their new faith hidden.

In addition to being exploited and underpaid, Asian and African foreign employees face daily verbal and physical abuse due to their race and low social standing. Being a Christian can make things worse. Expatriate Christians fear being detained and deported if they share their religion or gather to fraternize. However, the small number of Saudi Christians is constantly growing, and they are becoming more outspoken, sharing their religion with others through the Internet and Christian satellite television networks.

Access to Bibles.

Saudi Arabia is one of the most prohibitive and difficult places in the world for Christians, especially those who convert from Islam. Saudi Arabia has no formal churches at this time. Conversions from Islam are considered apostasy and are punishable by death according to Islamic law. On the other hand, Saudi converts are more likely to be killed by their relatives in "honor killings" than to be imprisoned or punished by the government.

Under the new visitor limitations, a Bible can be entered into the country for personal use only and does not contain objectionable information. A large number of Bibles should not be shown in public, and anyone caught with too many Bibles will face "serious repercussions." Needless to say, the possession of a Bible is very restricted in Saudi Arabia. Some Saudi searchers and converts are fully aware of the risk of owning a Bible and many use the Internet and other digital media to access Scripture.

To restrict debate and discussion and silence critics, the Saudi government continues to use criminal charges of apostasy and blasphemy as a tool of intimidation. These accusations are generally directed against defenders of political reforms and human rights and against those who wish to debate the relationship of religion with the State, its laws and society.

State-sponsored corporal punishment.

In February 2015, a Saudi man was allegedly sentenced to death by a General Court for apostasy. According to several sources, an anonymous individual uploaded to a social network a video in which he appeared destroying pages of the Koran while making derogatory statements about Muslims. The conviction and death penalty were supported by this film, which was presented as evidence in court.

Saudi writer, activist and founder of the Free Saudi Liberals website Raif Badawi was arrested in 2012 for "insulting Islam through electronic channels" and was charged with apostasy in court. After being convicted of several charges, in 2014 he was sentenced to ten years in prison, 1,000 lashes and a fine. According to the ruling, Badawi – founder and editor of a website that functioned as an online platform for users to express themselves freely – was sentenced to receive 50 weekly lashes for 20 consecutive weeks. On January 9, 2015, a volunteer gave Badawi the first batch of 50 lashes. Following the execution of Badawi's flogging sentence, several nations, especially the United States, numerous international human rights organizations and individuals expressed their opposition to the execution of the punishment. No more flogging has been administered to Badawi because of widespread global protest and, in part, because a medical specialist determined that Badawi could not physically tolerate further whipping. After serving ten years in Dhahban Central Prison in Saudi Arabia, Badawi was released from prison on 11 March 2022, serving his entire sentence.

In July 2014, Badawi's lawyer, Waleed Abulkhair, was sentenced by a Specialized Criminal Court to 15 years in prison on multiple baseless charges stemming from his work as an international human rights defender.

After being arrested on the pretext of drug charges and spending more than two years in prison without charge, Sultan Hamid Marzooq al Enezi and Saud Falih Awad al Enezi were two Saudi men released from prison in June 2014. Although no official charges were ever filed, reports indicated that the two men were being held on suspicion of having committed apostasy for having converted to the Ahmadi interpretation of Islam.

Those arrested and charged with witchcraft – a crime punishable by death – continued to be prosecuted.

According to the Saudi Ministry of Justice, by June 2014 prosecutors had filed 191 cases of alleged witchcraft between November 2013 and May 2014.

Following a 2003 witchcraft conviction that landed her on death row for more than ten years, Ati Bt Abeh Inan, an Indonesian domestic worker, received a life sentence that was commuted by King Abdullah in February 2014.

According to Saudi Arabia's official death figures, by the end of November 2015 one hundred and fifty-one people had been executed, the highest number of executions in a single year since 1995. One person was executed every two days on average due to the considerable increase in executions. According to official figures, between 79 and 90 people a year were beheaded in recent years for crimes that included non-lethal offences, such as those related to drugs.

Discrimination and persecution of Shia Muslims are widespread in Saudi Arabia. In April 2021, Saudi Arabia executed 37 people, the vast majority Shiites. One of them was imprisoned and nailed to a cross. According to the Kingdom, three of the criminals were minors at the time of committing their crimes.

According to some speculation, the increase in executions may be due to the Saudi authorities' desire to communicate loud and clear that the regime is stable and will not tolerate violations of the law following the 2011 uprising and calls for reform in the country, including those of the country's Shiite Muslim community. According to estimates, the Shia minority constitutes between 10 and 15 percent of the population.

As a consequence of the supposed words of the Prophet Muhammad, apostates are subject to the death penalty according to Islamic law. It remains legal for the Saudi government to detain and imprison those who express dissent, renounce their religious beliefs, blaspheme or practice witchcraft. A 2014 law classifies blasphemy and the preaching of atheism as acts of terrorism.

It seems that apostasy is more than just a conversion, and the law prohibiting it is actively applied in the country. One example is the 2012 blasphemy charge against Saudi Arabian novelist Hamza Kashgari for tweets expressing his personal religious views that appeared on Twitter. Although he first attempted to flee the country, he was arrested in Malaysia and returned to Saudi Arabia, where he was held in pre-trial detention. He was released nearly two years later, after apologizing for comments on Twitter.

According to another report, Saudi authorities imprisoned two people and accused them of committing apostasy for adhering to the Ahmadiyya interpretation of Islam.

During a crackdown on anti-government gatherings in the Shiite province of Qatif on 14 February 2012, Ali Mohammed al-Nimr was arrested at the age of 17 and charged with terrorism. Authorities accused him of participating in illegal protests and possessing a firearm without a permit, although there is no evidence to support his claims. The case against al-Nimr appears to be based on his family ties to his uncle Sheikh Nimr al-Nimr, a 53-year-old critic of the Saudi regime and a recognized Shiite leader in the kingdom who was executed on Jan. 2, 2015, according to the evidence presented. On 27 May 2014, after two years of deliberation, he was sentenced to "death by crucifixion". He had been sentenced to death as a child; but fortunately his sentence was commuted on October 27, 2021.

Although unusual, five Yemenis were convicted of armed robbery and murder in the remote Jizan region in November 2013 and subsequently sentenced to death by crucifixion after being convicted. The bodies of the decapitated Yemenis were shown in public.

When a criminal is publicly beheaded in Saudi Arabia, his body can be placed on a cross for up to three days as a public example to deter dissonance. According to the Islamic penal code, the specific offence of attacking and attacking civilians to inflict deliberate harm or death with the intention of intimidating them is punishable by death followed by crucifixion.

Currently, Saudi authorities administer tranquilizers to the culprits before transporting them in a police van to a public square or parking lot after Friday prayer at noon. Their eyes are covered and their eyes are blindfolded as a safety precaution. When the police have cleared the square of all traffic, a blue plastic sheet of about 4 square meters is spread on the ground. Their limbs are chained and their hands and arms are handcuffed behind their backs. An agent leads the prisoner to the center of the sheet, where he is forced to kneel facing Mecca and beheaded with a sword while still dressed and barefoot. The executioner wields a huge sword between shouts of "Allahu Akbar!" (Although beheadings are performed in public, it is strictly forbidden to photograph them. The publication of video footage of the execution of a woman in January 2015 led to the arrest of the perpetrator.

A Sunni man was reportedly beheaded and his body was publicly exposed after being nailed to a pole. While the Saudi government claims all executions were carried out in accordance with the law, Amnesty International has expressed concern about what it calls the country's "shocking wave of deaths." According to Amnesty International, 11 men have been convicted of spying for Saudi Arabia's archrival Iran. Instead, 14 others have been sentenced to death for allegedly committing "violent acts" by participating in anti-government protests against the Saudi government in 2011-2012.

Believe it or not, we live in the twenty-first century and witness a brutal Christian persecution similar to that suffered by the early church. However, these are the end-time sufferings that were prophesied to occur and will.

Let us pray for the safety of all Christians in Saudi Arabia and for continued wisdom and discernment in their quest to follow and share Jesus. According to the 2022 Open Door Watch List, it is the 11th most dangerous country for Christians to reside in, with an extreme level of risk.

Isn't it ironic that my good friend Pastor Yenny Gomez from Venezuela called me and expressed her desire to visit Saudi Arabia while writing this chapter?

And the clock keeps ticking, ticking, ticking...

CHAPTER 4

SUDAN

"Rejoice and rejoice, for your reward is great in heaven, for thus persecuted the prophets who preceded you." Matthew 5:12 (NIV)

*****

Sudan's civil war between North and South is intrinsically linked to the massive persecution of Christians in the country, especially in the South. This struggle has been fought intermittently since 1955, making it the longest civil war in the world, and it continues with little respite. Both diplomacy and international media attention have remained equally silent; meanwhile, the war has claimed a huge and tragic toll. More than two million people have died since the war began; these figures include the by-products of war, such as famine caused by conflict. Five million people have been displaced, and another half a million have sought refuge across the international border. Hundreds of thousands of women and children have been abducted and enslaved. By all accounts, it currently appears to be the world's worst humanitarian tragedy.

In this dispute, religion is the most important factor. The north, which accounts for nearly two-thirds of Sudan's surface area and population, is Muslim and Arabic-speaking; the identity of the north is a perfect blend of Islam and Arabic. In terms of ethnicity, culture and religion, the South is more indigenous; its identity is indigenous to Africa, with Christian influences and a Western orientation.

Although Christianity predated Islam in northern Sudan, it was completely eliminated and replaced by Islam in the early sixteenth century. The southern part of the country was then introduced into Christianity through missionary activities during British colonialism in the late nineteenth century. Since independence from the British, Arabization and Islamization programs have posed a danger to the south. Surprisingly, religious persecution of non-Muslims has the effect of promoting Christianity; as South Sudanese now see Christianity as the most effective means of combating the imposition of Islam, especially since traditional African religions are unable to resist the forces of spiritual and religious globalization.

Hope for Christians.

Since the overthrow of the murderous regime of Sudanese President Omar al-Bashir in 2019, Christians in that country have witnessed encouraging and hopeful developments toward religious freedom under the new transitional government. Although the country is ranked Number 13 on the Open Door World Watch List, there remains strong anti-Christian sentiment in many communities, promoted and supported by government policies that interfere with church activities. It is estimated that almost two million Christians live in Sudan, which has a total population of 43.5 million people, which is equivalent to about 4.5% of the total.

Although Sudan has made significant strides towards religious freedom, Christians of Muslim origin continue to suffer severe persecution by their families and communities in Sudan. Although these people no longer fear the death penalty for rejecting Islam, they may continue to be harassed, ostracized, or discriminated against in any way if their religious beliefs are discovered. Sadly, it is not uncommon for Christian churches and places of worship to be damaged, if not completely destroyed.

To ensure their protection and that of their family members, many people continue to keep their religious beliefs secret. Some converts are so concerned about retaliation from community leaders that they prefer not to raise their children as Christians. People of Muslim origin are more likely to perform Islamic burials in Muslim cemeteries because of this fear of exposure.

Attempted demolition of churches.

The Sudanese Christian Church has been the victim of church demolitions, property confiscations and unjust imprisonment; however, persecution of this kind has only increased in recent years.

First, the Khartoum Administrative Court oversaw a complaint that allegedly prevented the Sudanese government from demolishing 25 churches in the Khartoum region. According to the complaint, the 25 churches in Khartoum state had been designated for demolition in a letter sent on 13 June 2016 by the Government, Environment, Roads and Demolitions Of Irregularities Government Land Protection Corporation of Khartoum State, which alleged that the churches had been built on land that had been designated for another use. The Christian leaders who filed the complaint believed the decision was part of a broader and more systematic campaign to suppress Christianity across Sudan. In addition, in 2012, endowment ministry dissolved the democratically elected committee that oversaw church property since 1902 and replaced it with a corrupt commission that sold most of the church's land. The Board of Administration ruled in February 2015 that the ministry had no authority to appoint this commission, and that the elected committee had the legal authority to deal with church property. Sadly, the Sudanese government has refused to implement the court's verdict, allowing the corrupt commission to remain in power. Even now, the fake commission aims to profit from the sale of the church grounds when the buildings are demolished. Although she was willing to go ahead with her plans in February 2017, the churches filed an appeal to prevent the demolition. The matter was pending before the Khartoum Administrative Court, but was rejected, which was a disappointment for the Christian community. Five churches have already begun the process of appealing the verdict to a court of greater jurisdiction.

The Sudanese government has repressed the Christian community on multiple occasions, regularly interfering in their lands and places of worship. For example, Sudanese officials said in 2014 that new churches would not be allowed to be built.

Stop speaking on behalf of Christians.

On Friday, July 2, 2021, Sudan's Ministry of Religious Affairs and Endowments employee Botrous Badawi was attacked at midnight by four masked gunmen at a location south of the capital, Khartoum. Badawi, a Christian who works as an adviser to the director, testified that four armed men chased his vehicle before stopping in front of it and forcing him out. He was severely beaten and threatened with death if he continued to advocate for the return of the properties of the Evangelical Presbyterian Church of Sudan to Christians. The attackers were armed with AK-47 assault weapons. According to Badawi, one of the attackers told him that if he talked about the property of the Evangelical Presbyterian Church of Sudan again, he would be killed next time. Badawi explained that one of the assailants hit him with his rifle.

Before the incident, Badawi recalled receiving numerous threatening text messages, including "We will use means you may not like and confront you with all the weapons we have," one of the text messages read. In the end, Badawi suffered several injuries to various parts of the body, including numerous bruises and fractures as a result of the attack. He was hospitalized for treatment.

Badawi has continued to push for restitution of church property confiscated under the previous regime and has commented on the attack published in a local publication.

In Sudan, Christians are still waiting for the restitution of their property that the government took over during the Islamist rule of Omar al-Bashir, which was overthrown in April 2019.

Forced to hide.

During his time as a scrap dealer in Ameth's common market in Abyei, a 4,072-square-mile area on Sudan's border established as a result of the 2005 peace agreement that ended that country's civil war, Ahmed Alnour helped assist his wife and seven children in Sudan, where he currently resided next to them. Alnour, a tribal Arab man from Misseriya, would soon be forced to leave that job, after local Muslims confirmed that he had converted to Christianity.

On the afternoon of April 1, 2019, he witnessed and heard the perpetrators declare, "We will kill you because you left Islam and became an infidel." He recalled that they tried to set fire to his house that day. Although the neighbors were able to put out the fire without being damaged, the assailants returned at 1 a.m. on April 8. He was sleeping and when he woke up, his house was engulfed in flames.

Christians came to rescue him.

The Christians took him to a hospital the next morning for treatment. He claimed that although he lost everything in the fire, including 600,000 South Sudanese pounds (equivalent to 6,000 US dollars), Alnour maintains the firm conviction that he was protected after putting his trust in Christ. "I want to share my new trust in Jesus with my family, and I'm sure they will come to believe alongside me," Alnour said.

The dangers increase as Muslims continue to seek Christ. Fear of Muslim reactions in Sudan and a lack of economic opportunities prevent Alnour from returning home to his family. However, he hopes to return and share the gospel with them one day, he added.

Church building burned down.

According to Rev. Kuwa Shamal, head of mission of the Sudanese Church of Christ (SCOC), on January 3, 2021, a church building located in the rural district of Tambul, in Al Jazirah, southeast of Khartoum, was demolished by suspected Muslim extremists. An undetermined number of alleged assailants demolished the structure.

According to local church leaders, in the weeks leading up to the fire, which a group of individuals carried out, hateful comments directed at Christians were shared on social media.

SCOC pastor Jubrial Tutu denounced the arson, claimed it was a "direct persecution of Christians" and called for an investigation.

By the day of the assault, Sunday attendees had already left the building, according to Pastor Shamal. He said the attempted fire occurred just minutes after they left. According to the pastor, the building, which served congregations of various denominations, was the only Christian church of worship in the Tambul area.

According to morning Star News' interview with Pastor Shamal, the church was attacked because local residents did not want any trace of the cross in the area.

Some social media posts have urged Sudanese Muslims to reject any attempt by church officials to seek approval of properties to be used as church buildings. The presence of "infidel" properties, such as church buildings, should not be allowed in any Muslim city or village, one commentator claimed in January 2021. Another asked the Muslims of Tambul to prevent the construction of a second ecclesiastical structure in their city. "Do you want your church to be a miserable place when you build it in Tambul?" he asks in his letter to the mayor.

A defender of The rights and aid of Christians in Khartoum, Demas Mragan, claims that the church in Tambul was set on fire, marking the ninth time a Christian place of worship has been destroyed in the country since the beginning of 2019. Muslim extremists have threatened to kill members of the Christian congregation if they erect another temporary structure that would allow them to continue worship, according to the sources. In a messageto church leaders: "*If the government gives you permission to build a church here, you'd better be prepared to pick up your corpses.*"

Eighteen of the fourteen extremist Muslims who set fire to temporary prayer structures in the Dar El-Salam area of Omdurman, located across the Nile River from Khartoum, were captured by police in December, according to the lawyer representing the Christians. When interviewed, they said they did so because they did not want a Christian presence in the neighborhood.

Stand firm with the Sudanese.

Believers Middle East Concern asks you to take a firm stand in support of Sudanese believers. Support them in prayer and be aware of the difficulties they are going through. Pray that the government will refrain from harassing them, appropriating their property and demolishing their religious structures. Your congressional representatives can also help you speak on behalf of persecuted Christians in Sudan. The fact that there are people all over the world who pray for them, who think of them, who are aware of their situation and who do everything possible to help them, is fundamental for the church in Sudan.

Despite the persecutions, Sudanese Christians have gone from 1.6 million in 1980 to 11 million in 2010. However, 22 of the 24 Anglican dioceses operate in exile in Kenya and Uganda, and clergy receive no compensation for their services. Four million people remain internally displaced in Sudan, and another million live in Sudanese exile in other countries. These end-time persecutions have to take place as it wasperpetrated by the prophets.

"U.S. officials encouraged respect for religious freedom and the protection of minority religious groups. They urged the repeal of apostasy and blasphemy laws. They also stressed the need for a new and inclusive curriculum and urged government officials to refrain from the practices of the previous regime, which included the confiscation and demolition of religious property." (Source: US Dept. of State)

And the clock keeps ticking, ticking, ticking...

CHAPTER 5

SYRIA

"Be attentive; you will be handed over to the local councils and I will bescourged in the synagogues." Matthew 10:17

*****

The country of Syria has become a breeding ground for the persecution of Christians as a result of the country's ongoing civil war, which began in 2011. The nation's Christians have suffered tremendous disruption in their daily lives. They have been harassed and attacked from all sides and have been caught up in a horrible struggle between different Muslim factions. Since the beginning of the war, government actions have forced more than 750,000 Christian refugees to leave the nation. Throughout the war, the churches and Christians who have remained in Syria have acted as a beacon of hope and a source of calm for both Christians and Muslims. Many Muslims have converted to Jesus because Christians have reached out to them with acts of compassion and practical help. In addition, suggestions that neighboring nations could deport Syrian refugees back to Syria give Christians hope that people who have come to faith while in neighboring countries can return and help develop local churches.

Thousands of Christians have been internally displaced or sought refuge in neighbouring countries after more than a decade of war and the growth of Islamic extremism. In addition, the entry of the Turkish army into northern Syria at the end of 2019 aggravated the situation. On October 9, 2019, the Turkish Air Force entered the war and engaged in military operations by conducting airstrikes on border towns. More than 300,000 people have been displaced as a result of this violence, and more than 70 Syrian civilians and 20 Turks have died as a result. Amnesty International has also denounced human rights abuses.

In places under the influence of Islamic extremist groups such as ISIS, public demonstrations of Christianity are strictly prohibited, and the vast majority of churches have been confiscated or demolished altogether. In government-controlled areas this threat has diminished, but Islamic dissidents continue to abduct young Christians.

Surprisingly, the right of Christians in Syria to congregate for ecclesiastical and communal activities remains intact, albeit with some restrictions, due to the ongoing struggle to contain the spread of the COVID-19 virus. Christian pastors (and other religious leaders) have been excluded from travel restrictions to facilitate meetings with believers during the pandemic.

Although the government does not prohibit Christianity, some laws intentionally violate civil liberties. Some examples are the fact that a Muslim person cannot marry a Christian person. Moreover, if a parent converts from Muslim to Christian, the divorced Christian has no parental rights over the children shared with his or her former spouse.

Two especially dangerous threats to new Muslim-to-Christian converts are Islamic terrorists and members of the convert's own family. Conversion to Christianity is especially under pressure from Syrian families and communities, who believe that converting from Islam carries great shame. Some families have gone so far as to suggest that local officials continue to spy on Christian converts.

Christians fleeing.

There are currently 744,000 Christians living in Syria, down nearly 70,000 from 2021, and many are fleeing due to the threat of internally displaced persecution and suffering.

Although bloodshed has decreased in some parts of Syria, extremist Islamic groups continue to have authority over a significant part of the country's areas. Church leaders are especially vulnerable to kidnappings and kidnapping attempts.

Christians in the northeastern region of Syria are especially exposed to attacks by Islamic terrorists and the Turkish army. The Turkish army's operations in Syria and Iraq have too often resulted in the deaths of Christians, who have suffered greatly. In 2020, the Turkish intervention led to the displacement of 2,000 Christian families and the consequent depopulation of 25 Christian towns. Moreover, the Turkish military intervention in Syria is consistent with Turkey's anti-Christian sentiments, which include: continued discrimination and harassment against the Ecumenical Patriarchate and the remaining Christians in Turkey, along with the occupation and ethnic cleansing of northern Cyprus. Ironically, Turkey's history includes extensive Orthodox Christian baggage; however, many historical and iconic relics have become Muslim sites. For example, Hagia Sophia and the Monastery of the Holy Saviour in Chora, which were once Christian landmarks, have been converted into mosques. The numerous restrictions imposed on religious freedom are not limited to Turkey and Syria, but occur in many countries in the Middle East.

According to Kurdish media outlet Rudaw, around two-thirds of Syria's Christians have been forced to flee the war-torn country in the past ten years. Before the outbreak of civil conflict in 2011, Christians made up between 8 and 10 percent of Syria's population; they now account for about 3 percent of the population.

Syria's Christians reportedly took it upon themselves to provide assistance against Islamic State militants operating in the nation. According to data obtained by Rudaw, the Christian community in the Kurdish region of Jazira in northeastern Syria has shrunk from a population peak of about 150,000 people in 2011 to about 55,000.

Syria's Christians also have much to fear from the Free Syrian Army (FSA) jihadists, who have destroyed large numbers of churches and killed Christians. The FSA and several Islamist terrorist organizations have also released numerous videos showing them beheading Alawites, Shiite Muslims and Sunni Muslims loyal to the Syrian government, among other things. If you take into account the nature of Saudi Arabia and the fact that beheading is a legal punishment in this Muslim country, you can see how this parallels the barbarity of the FSA and Islamic terrorist networks.

When Islamic State forces took control of the Sinjar region in 2014, the Armenian genocide memorial church in Deir ez Zour is said to have been destroyed by an explosion caused by those forces. Unfortunately, Armenians found themselves in the midst of another conflict in the Middle East. Many Armenian-inhabited towns and villages in Syria were caught up in the fighting and some were even occupied by the Islamic State. As the war dragged on, many of Syria's cultural sites and places of worship were damaged, looted or even destroyed during the war, including many that were Armenian.

Repression is not new in Syria. Christians have at times been forced to flee persecution and massacre in areas controlled by the FSA and Islamist terrorist organizations.

Syria occupies a unique position in the biblical writings. The "Damascus Road" is a whimsical place where the apostle Paul converted to Christianity while traveling from Jerusalem. He wrote about stops in villages like Ma'loula, (an ancient shrine carved into a cliff on top of a mountain where residents still speak Aramaic, the language of Jesus) to convert residents to Christianity. However, these rich estates risk disappearing. Many ancient churches, once considered a safe haven from the tumult of the world, have been destroyed or left in a state of danger.

Many Christians who have dedicated their lives to the Lord have left Syria. In large part, those who remained have become even more dedicated to attending church services and working on their spiritual growth because of their experience.

Instead of focusing on activities or structures, the church learned that caring for people is at the core of its purpose. Thanks to this transformation of the mindset of church leaders, there has been a deeper interaction between church leaders and Christians.

Water weapon.

According to observers, Turkey and its Syrian militant partners have cut off the essential water supply of the Alok pumping station on August 13, 2020, for the ninth time since the invasion. Finally, they took control of the Ras al-Ain area in October 2019. As a result, they say, residents of Hassakeh, the region's largest city, are being drowned from their water supply and forced to submit.

The leader of the Syrian Orthodox Church, Patriarch Ignatius Aphrem II of Antioch, based in Damascus, has called on the peoples of the world to end Turkey's offensive operations in the region. Using water as a weapon is inhumane and a violation of fundamental human rights, he wrote in a letter to United Nations Secretary-General Antonio Guterres on August 21, 2021. However, despite repeated appeals from the people of the region, there has been no response from the international community to this atrocity.

The city of Afrin and the autonomous northeast have enjoyed the ability to choose their faith and religious beliefs until Islamist militants allied with the Turkish army invaded the area in January 2018. Since then, religious freedom has been restricted.

As a result of the persecution of Christians, Yazidis and other religious minorities have been forced to evacuate their homes, businesses and property. Many have been forced to flee their homeland. On the other hand, those who have converted to Christianity are especially vulnerable to Islamists.

Confiscation of Christian property.

The persecution of Christians in Syria continues; many Christians have fled, and those who remain are in a precarious situation due to the presence of jihadist groups within Christian communities.

Hungary's foreign minister expressed concern about "the fact that Christians are persecuted is being neglected in world politics," according to the Associated Press.

According to the Syrian Observatory for Human Rights (SOHR), in Idlib, Islamist militants have begun confiscating Christian property based on their religious convictions.

When it comes to imposing "Islamic sharia" on members of other religious communities, Christians in the Idlib region face injustice from jihadist organizations and transgressions from Islamic militias. According to the SOHR report, Islamist forces repress them and charge them a tax known as "Jizya" in an attempt to force them to leave their homes and move to regime-controlled areas.

According to the Syrian Observatory for Human Rights, jihadist rebels, in particular from Hay'at Tahrir Al-Sham (HTS), are pressuring Christian landowners to renew their

Lease agreements with their officers, which often causes them to have to increase the rent of their homes and businesses. According to SOHR, if a Christian landlord has fled jihadist-controlled territory, he is not allowed to retain ownership of his home.

Christians also have much to fear from the jihadists of the Free Syrian Army, who have destroyed a large number of Christian churches and killed Christians.

Christianity in Syria.

Syria was once considered a model of religious tolerance compared to most countries in the Middle East. However, in recent years, Syrian Christians have suffered the same restrictions and hostility that are widespread in the region's most restrictive countries as most Islamist countries, according to Christian leaders. For example, Christians frequently lose their jobs, homes, social standing, and family relationships due to religious persecution. The religious freedom of those born in Christian homes is guaranteed as long as they keep their faith to themselves, but Christians who share the gospel with others risk reprisals from extremists and sometimes the government.

Churches strive to meet the needs of the large number of internally displaced persons in the world. Despite the dangers and harsh conditions, some Christians have chosen to remain in the country to bear witness to Christ and spread the gospel. Syria is ranked Number 15 on the 2022 Open Doors Global Watch List and is rated "Very High Persecution."

Currently, the church in Syria believes that its mission is to communicate to people around the world that the root cause of their distress is conflict and the lack of God in their lives. In addition, the church wishes to announce to people that nothing in life can bring them true joy except a restored connection with Jesus Christ.

Support Syrian Christians.

Let us pray that Syrian Christians may return to their homes, families, communities and workplaces. Pray that God will continue to restore those who have already returned to their homes and villages. Pray that Syrian believers will serve as a beacon of hope in their country, providing comfort and guidance to those suffering from trauma or lack of food or resources. Let us pray that the Word of God will permeate the land of Syria and that believers will be filled with new joy, strength and hope as a result of their reflection on it. Let us pray that, like the apostle Paul, Syria will set out on the "Damascus Road" and have an encounter with the one true God.

According to the International Society for Human Rights, although Christians make up about 30% of the world's population, they are subject to approximately 80% of acts of religious discrimination.

And the clock keeps ticking, ticking, ticking...

Iraq

CHAPTER 6

IRAQ

"Rejoice and rejoice, for your reward is great in heaven, for thus persecuted the prophets who preceded you." Matthew 5:12

*****

According to historical sources, the Christians of Iraq are one of the oldest Christian groups in the world, existing since the first century A.D. Most Iraqi Christians are ethnic Assyrians of Eastern Aramaic. According to the Iraqi Christian Association, they are descended from the inhabitants of ancient Assyria and adhere to the Syriac Christian tradition. In addition to their ethnic identity, several religious denominations are known by the names of their religious confessions, as well as by their ethnic identities, such as Chaldean Catholics, the Syrian Orthodox Church or Chaldean Catholics. Iraqi Christians who are not of Assyrian descent are overwhelmingly Arab and Armenian Christians, with a small minority of Kurdish, Shabak and Turkmen Iraqi believers. Most of today's Iraqi Christians of Assyrian descent are ethnically, linguistically, historically, and genetically distinct from the Kurds, Arabs, Iranians, and Turkmens, among other groups in Iraq. It doesn't matter what subsection of Christian affiliation you have because Eastern Aramaic-speaking Christians in and around Iraq are genetically similar. They are considered a distinct people with origins and history dating back to ancient Assyria and Mesopotamia, respectively. Assyrian Christians are also found in northern and eastern Syria, in southern and eastern Turkey, in northern and western Iran, and in the world's largest diaspora.

Syrian Christianity was first established in Mesopotamia. Some subgroups of Syriac Christians settled in northern and south-central Iraq, where they would later spread to become one of the most popular Christian churches in the Middle East, the Fertile Crescent region, and even India and China.

Iraq has made a significant and lasting contribution to Christian history. It is the country with the most biblical history, second only to Israel, of all the countries in the world. In southern Iraq, Patriarch Abraham was from Uruk, now known as Nasiriyah, and matriarch Rebekah was from Assyria in northwestern Iraq. In addition, Daniel spent most of his life in Iraq. The prophet Ezekiel was originally from southern Iraq, and his sanctuary can still be found there. Other shrines are dedicated to the prophet Jonah, St. George, and several other biblical prophets and saints have origins in the area. Many theorize that Adam, Eve, and the biblical Garden of Eden were created in southern Iraq.

SIGNS OF THE TIMES: *THE GREAT PERSECUTION*

Christianity in Iraq.

Christians have lived in Iraq for a few hundred years, after the death and resurrection of Christ. The historic Christian community has lived throughout Iraq and has been concentrated mainly in the north of the country. They identify closely with Christianity and use the Bible as a framework for establishing their communities; so much so that they perceive themselves as a people and an independent country. That sense of national identity and connection to the north predates the arrival of Christianity. It serves as the basis for their claim to be the indigenous people of Iraq.

Following the overthrow of Saddam Hussein in 2003, Iraq has finally achieved an unstable peace; recently, the country has witnessed a resurgence of violent uprisings. The country's volatility serves as a trigger for the continued persecution of Christians.

Overall, Iraq has an insecure environment with a bleak outlook for the future. In the Middle East, Christianity is not necessarily on the way to disappearing; there is a chance that stabilising measures will be successful. However, given the state of events, it is difficult to foresee a viable and sustainable future for Iraq's Christian residents.

Christian persecution.

Because of the pressure and dangers that Christians of Muslim origin may suffer from extended family members and local clan leaders (or sheikhs), many of them are forced to keep their new faith in a closely guarded secret. Christian converts risk losing their inheritance rights and their right to marry: they would not be allowed to marry Christians because the law would consider them Muslims, as their conversion was covert.

Christian communities continue to be targeted and abducted by Islamic extremists in Iraq. They are discriminated against by the government in a variety of areas, ranging from the workplace to border checkpoints. The government can use sharia against those who strive to spread the gospel, among others.

The hostility and persecution of many Christians has a profoundly negative effect on their lives. The vast majority of those responsible for this hostility are extremist Islamic organizations and non-Christian leaders. They are also discriminated against at the hands of government officials. Iraq is ranked No. 14 on the 2020 Open Door Global Watch List. This is due to an increase in the number of reports of church closures from Turkish attacks in northern Iraq, as well as in the number of Christians who have been kidnapped.

According to population statistics from the Shlama Foundation, in 2003, just before the U.S. invasion of Iraq, an estimated 1.2 million Christians lived there. The 2020 figure is about less than 250,000, representing an eighty percent decline in less than two decades. If this trend continues, a centuries-old religious minority in Iraq will disappear altogether.

According to official estimates, the exodus of half of the country's Christian population would have been driven by the demolition of 243 cathedrals and churches and the murder of pregnant women and children. Due to persecution, almost all Iraqi Christians have migrated to Kurdistan from the Arab regions of Iraq. The vast majority of Iraqi Christians now reside in Kurdistan, in the country's northernmost province. Between 2003 and 2016, most of the refugees from Kurdistan were internally displaced from Arab nations who were forced to flee their homes due to various wars and crises. According to the United Nations, Christian Arabs, especially those fleeing targeted attacks, have little difficulty entering the Kurdistan Region. However, they have difficulty getting their refugee status approved by the Central Administration in Baghdad.

An estimated 330,000 people travelled to Syria, with a smaller number heading to Jordan. Thousands of people fled to Iraqi Kurdistan, located in northern Iraq, and to neighboring nations such as Iran. Christians who cannot leave their ancestral lands have mainly made their way to Erbil, especially the Christian suburb of Ainkawa, located within the city. In addition, more than 10,000 Iraqi Christians, mainly from Assyria, live in the UK, led by Archbishop Athanasios Dawood, who has urged the government to take in more refugees.

Aside from emigration, the number of Iraqi Christians is declining due to a lower birth rate and a higher mortality rate than their Muslim counterparts. Since the invasion of Iraq, Islamic extremist organizations have targeted Assyrians and Armenians, and other religious minorities.

In the historic city of Mosul in 2007, Father Ragheed Aziz Ganni and subdeacons Basman Yousef Dawid,

Wahid Hanna Esho and Gassan Isam Bidawed of the Chaldean Catholic Church were killed. It was discovered that Ganni and his three deacons were kidnapped, forced to convert to Islam and subsequently executed when they refused. Ganni belonged to the Chaldean Church of the Holy Spirit in Mosul and graduated in 2003 in ecumenical theology from the Pontifical University of St. Thomas Aquinas, Angelicum in Rome. He was previously pastor of the Chaldean Church of the Holy Spirit in Mosul. He was previously pastor of the Chaldean Church of the Holy Spirit in Mosul.

Six months after his assassination, on 29 February 2008 Paulos Faraj Rahho, archbishop of Mosul, was kidnapped and killed along with his bodyguards and driver. They were discovered buried near the city of Mosul and later identified.

On October 31, 2010, a terrorist attack took place on the Syrian Catholic Cathedral in Baghdad, Iraq, during Sunday night Mass at the Cathedral of Our Lady of Salvation. At least 58 people were killed in the incident, which came after more than 100 people were taken hostage. The Islamic State of Iraq, a Sunni insurgent group affiliated with al Qaeda, claimed responsibility for the attack; however, Shiite cleric Ayatollah Ali al-Sistani, among others, denounced the attack.

In 2013, Assyrian Christians returned to their historic lands on the Nineveh Plains, including Mosul, Erbil and Kirkuk. Assyrian militias were then formed to safeguard towns and cities against invasion.

In July 2014, while conducting a campaign in northern Iraq, the Islamic State of Iraq issued a decree requiring all indigenous Assyrian Christians in the area under its control to leave the lands the Assyrians had inhabited for more than 5,000 years, to pay a special tax of about $470 per family. that they converted to Islam or were killed. Many of them sought safety in the Kurdish-controlled areas of Iraq that were nearby. The homes of Christians have been painted with the Arabic letter nn, meaning Nassarah (Arabic word for Christian), as well as with a statement that they are "owned by the Islamic State." On July 18, 2020, ISIS fighters appeared to have changed their minds and proclaimed that all Christians would have to flee or face execution. Islamic terrorists stole the precious objects of the vast majority of individuals who were forced to flee.

Inconvenience.

Extermination, forced displacement, torture and brutality operations have been perpetrated against Iraqi Christians, who have become targets of Sunni Islamist groups such as al Qaeda and ISIS. Iraqi Christians fled the country after the 2003 Iraq war, and its population has plummeted, from some 1.2 million Christians to fewer than 250,000 in 2020, due to failed efforts by the democratic government to restore order. The vast majority of Christians have migrated to Iraqi Kurdistan or taken refuge in other parts of the world.

In addition to being tragic for local Christian communities and for the Church in general, as a consequence of the disappearance of Christianity in its place of origin, the almost complete eradication of Christianity in Iraq should raise serious concerns about the situation of Christians in other countries whose governments may look to Iraq as an example of how to treat the unwanted Christ. Moreover, this persecution has ramifications beyond the immediate impact on Christians. Countries that have proven to be enemies of a minority group are likely to have no qualms about persecuting and eradicating other minority groups and religions that they perceive as impediments to their national and religious goals. Therefore, in the midst of this terrible reality for Iraqi Christians, the situation of Christians and others throughout the area cannot and should not be ignored.

In the Middle East, Christians are too often regarded as an unwanted minority, which is unfortunate. You don't have to look far to recognize this fact. The problem is that they are not just an unwanted minority; they are being actively persecuted and killed in Iraq in an attempt to establish an all-Islamic sphere of influence, and those who want them to leave are succeeding in their efforts to eliminate them.

Pray for Christians in Iraq.

Let us pray for the safety and tranquility of workers smuggling Bibles to neighboring nations, Christian converts from Islam in Baghdad, where persecution has increased, and the expansion of house churches in Kurdish areas.

According to Pew Research, between 2007 and 2014, Christians have been subjected to harassment in more countries than any other religious group.

And the clock keeps ticking, ticking, ticking...

CHAPTER 7

INDIA

"Then you will be delivered to persecution and death, and you will be hated by all nations because of me." Matthew 24:9

*****

According to historical records, since the introduction of Christianity in India around the first millennium, Hindus and Christians have historically coexisted in relative peace. The introduction of European colonialists in the eighteenth century gave rise to a wave of missionary activity in southern and northeastern India, which continues today.

In recent decades, many indigenous civilizations have converted to Christianity, sometimes voluntarily and sometimes violently and forcibly. One example is the Goan Inquisition, responsible for the forced conversion of Hindus, Muslims and Jews throughout India between 1560 and 1812. (The Goan Inquisition is widely recognized as the most brutal act of religious persecution ever carried out by the Portuguese Catholic

Church. It was essentially a genocide perpetrated against the Indian people. Thousands of people were tortured and killed if they refused to convert.)

In India, Christian missionaries working under British control have been accused of forcibly preaching, sparking hostility toward Hindus and Muslims during the nineteenth century. There is a possibility that this contributed to the Indian Rebellion, also called the First War of Independence of 1857, against British rule in India.

Many Christian principles fostered reform movements within Hindu culture in the nineteenth century, the most important of which was the Brahmo Samaj, which was influenced by British Christian unilateralism and was the most notable of these movements. The Brahmo Samaj conceived the future religion of India as a mixture of Christianity and Hindu philosophies.

In most cases, Hindus who converted to Christianity maintained their social conventions, including caste practices, with minor exceptions. Indian Christians have preserved Hindu traditions and rituals, while combining Hindu traditions and practices with Christianity to create a style of Indian Christianity unlike any other. For example, the Hindu celebration of Diwali is celebrated by a large number of Christians in India. As a result of this kind of syncretism, the Christian churches of India are faced with a confusing situation, which makes it necessary to study the theologically the interface between Hinduism and Christianity. Indian Christians, for the most part, have rejected religious exclusivism and have decided to peacefully coexist alongside Hindus in their country.

In more recent times, the friendship between Hindus and Christians has been tested by the politics of parties and the radicalism of members of both religious communities. In the wake of Christian missionary activities among lower-caste Hindus, crypto-Christians have emerged, mainly among Dalits and other lower-caste Hindus. Discrimination against Dalit Christians has persisted among Catholics in India, especially among the Christian clergy of the upper castes, and is still present in some ecclesiastical sectors.

There has been a backlash against Christianity by the Hindu majority in four Indian states (Rajasthan, Madhya Pradesh, Himachal Pradesh and Tamil Nadu, to name a few), which have passed laws restricting or prohibiting conversion to Christianity. The Indian Christian community has expressed great discontent with this. Right-wing Hindu groups have been accused of attacking pastoralists and preventing them from holding religious services.

Hindu fundamentalists believe that all Indians should be Hindus and that the country should be cleansed of Christianity and Islam. They employ extreme violence to achieve their goal, with special emphasis on ancient Hindu converts to Christianity. Christians are accused of practicing a "foreign religion" and held accountable for "bad luck" in their communities. Christian converts are routinely beaten and, in some cases, subjected to constant pressure from their families and communities to return to Hinduism or even be killed. They may suffer a boycott of their community if they don't "reconvert," which would have a terrible impact on their ability to make a living and support their family. Many Christians are isolated and have little communication with other believers.

COVID-19 and anti-Christian propaganda.

On May 31, 2021, Indian police arrested four members of a Christian family and put them in prison. According to local sources, the four Christians were accused of violating COVID-19 lockdown rules and state anti-conversion laws, instilled by extremist Hindu nationalists, for doing nothing but gathering in their private homes to pray.

International Christian Concern is collecting data on persecution across India. They have observed where hardline Hindu nationalists are using the pandemic as a weapon against Christians. Christians have been unfairly accused of violating COVID-19 protocols in several cases. In other cases, Christians are associated with outrageous conspiracy theories about the pandemic to foment hatred and fear.

Dr Sandhya Tiwary, a Christian, participated in medical visits to patients in Baina, a village in Madhya Pradesh, on May 22, 2021. He visited COVID-19 patients who received door-to-door medical care. Dr. Tiwary was falsely accused of engaging in illegal conversion activities by Hindu radicals. They then recorded a video in which he appeared praying for the sick, which they distributed on the Internet. In response to the controversy over the false accusation, the Madhya Pradesh state government suspended Dr Tiwary.

Dr. Tiwary responded by creating a video of her own, which garnered a lot of attention on social media. "What's wrong with informing them that God is healing them?" he asked. "I never told or forced anyone to become a Christian, nor did I pressure anyone to pray to Jesus. All I told them was that Jesus heals."

According to another incident, Indian TV yoga guru Acharya Balkrishna tweeted that the COVID-19 protests are a "conspiracy to convert the whole country to Christianity and at the same time turn them against yoga and Ayurveda." According to the tweet, Balakrishna essentially blamed Christians for the devastating outbreak of the epidemic and encouraged people to buy Ayurvedic medicines and traditional Indian treatments produced by Balakrishna and Baba Ramdev, to combat COVID-19.

However, Dr. J.A. Jeyalal, president of the Indian Medical Association (IMA), stated that the IMA had not demonstrated the medical value of Ayurveda in the fight against COVID-19. Dr. Jeyalal, also a Christian, was the next person to fall victim to the anti-Christian propaganda machine of COVID-19.

A law firm sued Dr. Jeyalal for allegedly using IMA's platform to "promote Christianity." The court ordered Dr. Jeyalal to refrain from writing, speaking on any media platform or publishing any defamatory content against Hinduism or Ayurveda.

In the face of this challenging wave of the pandemic, Indians have generally come together to help each other survive. This situation has been substantive regardless of caste, color, creed or even religious affiliation. The statement "humanity is in full swing" is frequently heard among neighbors who support each other.

Radical Hindu nationalists, by contrast, continue to harass Christians in India with false criminal charges and spread insane conspiracy theories. Amid the pandemic, radicals have politicized COVID-19 protocols and promoted anti-Christian narratives about the virus to advance their goal of transforming India into a Hindu nation, as Reuters reports.

Persecution can affect all areas of public and private life, and anti-conversion legislation (which already exists in 13 of India's 29 states at the time of writing) is used to harass and intimidate Christians. Although only a small number of people are convicted under these statutes, the legal process can be an economic burden and drag on for years.

While persecution has increased dramatically in India over the previous five years, it has remained relatively stable since the end of 2020. The COVID-19 pandemic has provided persecutors with a new weapon; Christians are often not taken into account when providing food and official COVID-19 aid. Many people have suffered food insecurity because of this, mainly because many Christians belong to the Dalit caste, so they are relatively impoverished, and have lost their sources of income.

As a result of the pandemic, several churches in India have moved to the top of the health and social care rankings of their immediate communities. However, evangelicals are concerned that greater freedom has been given to the spread of disinformation and violence against religious minorities.

Powerful forces against Christians.

According to international organizations such as the World Evangelical Alliance and Open Doors, Christians and Muslims have been stigmatized in the country's media due to the spread of false information.

The Evangelical Fraternity of India (EFI) has published its semi-annual report on hatred and targeted violence against Christians in India, published in the second half of 2020. According to the organization, there have been 145 episodes of religious persecution against the Christian minority, of which three have been fatal. There are strong forces willing to confront the Christian presence in India. Even before the year 2021 has passed halfway, several of India's most powerful groups began planning ways to combat the Christian presence in the country, with debates and announcements on how to rid the country of "padri" (the Hindi word for Christian priest, pastor or clergy). As a result, they explain that ruthless and widespread violence erupted, ranging from murder to attacks on churches, false cases, impunity and police collusion, and social exclusion or boycott, now normalized, which are spreading like wildfire.

Violence against Christians by non-state actors in India is the result of a climate of selective hatred. India's governmental structure has created an atmosphere of impunity, which has fueled the translation of hatred into violence.

In addition, the hostility, intimidation and physical violence that Indian Muslims have suffered due to their conversion to Christianity are also well documented. Converts from Islam in India who become Christians are mistreated and rejected by their family. In addition, they may be tortured or killed by members of their clan or tribe, government officials, or extremist groups. In 2006, a Christian convert named Bashir Tantray was allegedly killed by Islamist militants in Kashmir's Kulgam district.

K.K. Alavi, a Christian priest, has received multiple death threats and criticized members of his former Muslim flock. An Islamic terrorist organization, known as the "National Development Front," has waged a sustained campaign against him. Reverend Alavi continues to receive threatening letters from radical organizations such as Tiger Force and the Islamic Front. In addition, the cross in front of his church was removed after it was attacked on multiple occasions.

The "threat" of prayer.

On July 28, 2021, a mob of extremist Hindu nationalists savagely attacked a preacher and his wife with an iron chain and wooden sticks. The attack occurred in the Indian state of Karnataka, and the pastor was knocked out and sent to hospital for treatment.

Pastor Shalem Maniraj and his wife visited the village of Doddahassala to pray for a sick church member. A score of hardline Hindu nationalists pounced on the couple as they arrived at the church member's house. The radicals used derogatory words towards the couple and accused them of converting others to Christianity.

Sensing the danger, Pastor Maniraj and his wife decided to leave the village immediately. Unfortunately, the mob attacked them as they left the village. Pastor Maniraj was beaten with an iron chain and wooden sticks until he fainted. Pastor Maniraj's wife was also beaten by the mob as she tried to defend her husband.

As the onslaught continued, a passing motorist stopped and rescued Pastor Maniraj and his wife. This individual took them to a neighboring hospital for urgent care.

In another incident, a pastor from the Indian state of Madhya Pradesh was savagely beaten by hardline Hindu nationalists. According to the media, the radicals claimed that the pastor was trying to convert destitute tribal people to Christianity through coercion.

Asia News reports claim that the Pastor of Tichkiya, only known as Bharat, was severely assaulted by extremist Hindu nationalists while holding a prayer meeting with three other Christians at his home. In their accusations, the radicals claimed that Pastor Bharat was "inciting" members of the indigenous tribal population to convert to Christianity. They attacked him and damaged his prayer center after a violent altercation between the two groups.

In response to the extremists' claim, Sajan K. George, president of the World Council of Indian Christians, told Asia News that the only thing Pastor Bharat possesses is the good news. "He distributes this freely to anyone who is willing to listen to him, and it is for this reason that he has been singled out to be attacked." George lamented that "Pentecostal Christians have unfortunately been the object of a violent campaign in many states of India."

On March 8, 2021, at a Christian worship session in central India, a crowd using knives, stones and wooden sticks launched a savage attack on the congregation, injuring several people. At least eight Christians were injured and taken to hospital as a result of the incident. According to local sources, the attack took place in Bastar district in the Indian state of Chhattisgarh. The attack began at approximately 7 p.m., when a crowd of 30 men led by a man named Ando Guddi broke into a house-church where 150 Christians had gathered for worship. Christians were attacked with axes, stones and wooden sticks after the mob broke into the house. To justify their attack, the mob invented a story that Christians performed illegal religious conversions. Many Christians were injured, and eight of them suffered serious injuries that required medical treatment. The mob also set fire to several bicycles and a motorcycle belonging to Christians.

Persecution increases.

Persecution has increased dramatically in India over the past five years and has lately remained virtually stable over the past year. Persecution of Christians has increased due to the COVID-19 epidemic, and Christians are frequently forgotten when food and official aid are delivered. Many Indians have been driven into despair by the lack of food, especially since many Christians belong to the Dalit caste. As a result, they are very impoverished and this year have seen their sources of income wiped out. According to Open Doors USA, India is currently the tenth most dangerous country to be a Christian in 2021.

Don't let your heart be troubled. The persecution of Christians is one of the many signs of the end times that are prophesied before the return of Jesus Christ.

And the clock keeps ticking, ticking, ticking...

Nigeria

CHAPTER 8

NIGERIA.

"Remember the word I said to you, 'A slave is no greater than his master.' If they persecuted me, they will also persecute you; if they kept my word, they will also keep yours." John 15:20

*****

In 2021, Nigeria is the country with the highest number of Christians killed for their religious beliefs. A common occurrence in the belts of northern and central Nigeria are violent attacks by Boko Haram and other Islamic extremist groups, including muslim militant herdsmen Hausa Fulani and ISWAP (an AFFILIATE of ISIS). These attacks are also becoming more frequent in the southern and eastern regions of the country.

As a result of these acts of brutality, Christians are frequently killed or their property and livelihoods destroyed. Most of the time, men and boys are at greater risk of being killed. The women and children left behind are incredibly vulnerable and serve as living testimony to the might of the assailants. In many cases, Christian women are kidnapped and raped by these barbaric groups, and are sometimes forced to marry Muslims. Unfortunately, the perpetrators of atrocities are rarely brought to justice.

Almost half of Nigerians are Christians – 95.4 million individuals out of a total population of 206.2 million – but most of them live in the southern regions of the country. Northern Nigeria is predominantly Muslim, and it is in the northern and central regions of the country that Christians suffer the worst persecution. It is well documented that violent attacks are most prominent in these northern and central belt regions.

Christians who have converted from Islam are especially vulnerable in the northern regions of the country, especially in areas under sharia jurisdiction. Relatives of Christians of Muslim origin often reject them and try to pressure them to convert again. When they do not convert again, many new Christians are expelled from their communities and removed from their livelihoods. As a result, many have few options and are forced to become internally displaced, and many settle in informal IDP camps. These Christians continue to suffer despite the harshness of the first persecution.

During Muhammadu Buhari's presidency (as of 2015), there has been a significant increase in attempts to force the Islamization of the country, including the appointment of Muslims to key government positions. As a result of the government's efforts to Islamize the country, even the Christian areas of the south are subject to persecution and violence. Christians who are internally displaced are also particularly susceptible.

Christian martyrdom.

In the first four months of 2021, "the number of Christians killed in Nigeria from January to April 2021 is 1,470, with Fulani herdsmen being responsible for more than 800," according to a report by Intersociety. 2,200 were kidnapped in that same period of time.

As the weather ticked by in Nigeria, things only got worse throughout the year. *"Jihadist Fulani herdsmen are responsible for the majority of the killings, with at least 1,909 deaths of Christians in 200 days,"* according to the Intersociety report. Boko Haram, ISWAP and Muslim Fulani bandits killed 1,063 Christians together, while the Nigerian army, assisted by Nigerian police and other branches of the armed forces, was responsible for 490 deaths of Christians. Another 300 Christians have died in captivity since the beginning of the conflict; at that time, for every 30 Christians kidnapped, an average of three Christians died. Another 150 Christians died as a result of what are known as "dark crime figures" or individuals who have died, but their death had not yet been officially reported or recorded.

In the first six months of 2021 it was reported that Islamic militants had "hacked to death" 3,462 Christians in the African nation. The figure was only 68 fewer than the total number of Christians killed in Nigeria in 2020. At the time, the number of Christians killed in Nigeria averaged 17 people a day.

According to a report by the International Society for Civil Liberties and the Rule of Law (Intersociety), by the end of 2021 some 3,462 Christians had been killed by Fulani and Boko Haram militants in Nigeria. Again, keep in mind that this was only the amount of destruction caused by Fulani and Boko Haram in 2021.

At the end of 2021, Intersociety published a report stating that the persecution had only worsened over time. According to official figures, 1,992 Christians had been killed between May 1 and July 18, 2021.

According to figures published by Open Doors, in 2021 there were 4,650 deaths of Christians. This figure was dangerously close to the numbers of 2014, in which there were more than 5,000 murders of Christians.

In the first three months of 2022, some 900 Nigerians died in violent incidents. Among the dead were hundreds of Christians, killed for their religious beliefs.

Regrettably, many of those guilty of anti-Christian carnage in the country have continued to evade justice and have been left unchecked, unfollowed, uninvestigated and without trial, leading to impunity and other atrocities against Christians in the country. The Nigerian government has also turned a deaf ear to the surviving victims and their families, who have been overwhelmingly abandoned. Following the killings and their oversight, the Nigerian government has faced harsh criticism and strong accusations of guilt and complicity from local communities as well as the international community.

Kidnappings.

In addition to an increase in the number of reported murders, 2021 saw a significant increase in the number of reported kidnappings. Since January 2021, an estimated 3,000 Christians have been kidnapped, according to reports. According to the research, it is likely that one in ten of them died, adding another 300 to the total death toll. In addition, the report adds 150 to the total to take into account the "dark figures", which are homicides that have not been reported or have not been detected so far.

Because extremists have targeted them, churches have been unable to offer people shelter. It is estimated that in 2021, 300 churches were attacked, destroyed, burned or threatened, and ten priests or pastors were kidnapped or killed by jihadists in these attacks.

Christians in the spotlight.

On March 7, 2021, pre-dawn attacks reportedly occurred in three villages near Jos, in Nigeria's Plateau State. The clashes killed people on both sides, and the death toll rose to 40.

The attacks were associated with members of the Muslim Fulani tribe, who are engaged in pastoralism, against members of the Berom Christian tribe, predominantly farmers.

As Christians tried to flee from the gunmen burning down village homes and churches, many of the victims, including women and children as young as 4 days old, were hacked to death. Others perished in their homes engulfed in flames.

This attack was a reflection of another that occurred in January, when intercommunal violence took place in the same neighborhood of the city.

In Kaduna State, located in the northwestern region of Nigeria, on June 19, 2022, shooters attacked not one, but two churches, Maranatha Baptist Church and St. Moses Catholic Church.

The shooters were reportedly responsible for the deaths of three people and the kidnapping of more than thirty. In addition to the kidnappings, the attack targeted four surrounding villages, causing the inhabitants of those villages to lose their homes. It has been established that those responsible for the violence are radicalized Fulani Islamic extremists.

When the attacks began, churches were holding their services. The three villagers killed were members of the local Catholic parish, although most of the kidnappings occurred at the local Baptist church.

The Kaduna State administration confirmed the three killings and stated that the assailants "broke into the communities on motorcycles." Investigations are currently underway to find the assailants, and security patrols are underway in the region.

Humanitarian crisis.

An escalation of a humanitarian disaster is taking place in northern Nigeria. Nigerians have been displaced from their homes in large numbers by terrorism perpetrated by Fulani terrorists and Boko

Haram, who have killed thousands of people. For these families, food, water, shelter and other basic human needs are in short supply due to lack of resources. On a daily basis, Nigerian Christians face terrorism, religious persecution and human rights violations across the country. It is high time to educate the public about these issues and provide help when needed. Nigeria must regain its balance quickly and not only for its own internal stability.

Nigeria is not alone in its crisis. Nigeria's destabilization and turmoil have spread to neighbouring countries, with more than 300,000 Nigerian refugees seeking refuge in Cameroon, Chad and Niger. As a result of extreme food insecurity and lethal terrorist attacks, the entire region is in a state of emergency. The geopolitical ramifications of an insecure Nigeria are serious and imminent.

In addition, Nigerian instability poses a national security problem for the United States and other Western countries. While ISIS may be losing ground in the Middle East, it has discovered a powerful new ally in northern Nigeria, Boko Haram. Like Afghanistan, Iraq and Syria, an unstable Nigeria is becoming a new breeding ground for Islamist terrorists. In the wake of December's International Religious Freedom Act, Nigeria became the first democratic nation to be added to the U.S. State Department's list of "countries of particular concern."

Nigeria is the third most terrorized country in the world, behind Afghanistan and Iraq, according to the Global Terrorism Index. According to their research, approximately 22,000 people were killed in terrorist attacks between 2001 and 2019.

Seventh worst country for a Christian.

On the Global Watch List, Nigeria has climbed several rungs and persecution has worsened across the board in both the public and commercial sectors. The violent attacks on Christians carried out by Boko Haram, Fulani militants, ISWAP (West Africa Province of the Islamic State) and other unidentified armed attackers have caused immense suffering among the Christian community.

Nigeria was elevated to No. 7 on the Global Watch List by 2022 because the previously isolated violence intensified and spread to new parts of Nigeria. The government is unable or unwilling to defend the religious freedom of its citizens and, consequently, attacks by Islamic extremists have continued unabated during the COVID-19 outbreak. Many Christians who have chosen to stay home to stop the virus have been targeted by terrorists. The vulnerability of many Christians who stay at home to prevent the spread of the virus has been exposed.

Death tolls published by the media or the government are approximate and often distorted due to the lack of a competent official record.

The number of Christians killed in Nigeria in 2021 exceeded the total number of Christians killed in Nigeria in 2020, which was 3,530, according to Christian persecution watchdog Open Doors.

Benue State, according to Intersociety, had the most significant number of Christian deaths recorded in 2021, with 450 deaths. According to the group, Kaduna State ranked secondwith 410 deaths of Christians.

Many people have accused the Nigerian government of not doing enough to protect its citizens. According to the Intersociety report, "the Nigerian government has continued to face harsh criticism and strong accusations of guilt and complicity in the killings and oversight of them." "The country's security forces have tested themselves and compromised to the point that they rarely intervene when defenseless Christians are threatened or attacked, but only appear after those attacks to arrest and incriminate the same targeted or persecuted community." According to advocates, insurgent groups often receive no consequences for their crimes or receive ransoms for kidnappings, even though the government denies ransoms to terrorists.

Nigeria, Africa's most populous country, is ranked No. 9 on Open Door's Global Christian Persecution Watch List in 2021, due to "grave" Islamic tyranny. "It is very sad that those responsible for the anti-Christian carnage in the country have been left without control, without follow-up, without investigation and without trial, which has led to impunity and the repetition of atrocities," Intersociety points out in the study. "The Nigerian government has also completely abandoned the surviving victims and the families of the deceased victims."

According to the US-based Christian persecution watchdog group International Christian Concern, jihadist attacks in West Africa have increased since the beginning of 2021, with Nigeria being the most targeted country in the region. In recent years, Islamic terrorist groups have killed thousands of people in the region as they seek to establish a caliphate and implement Islamic Sharia law.

"Christians have been the object of special attention and have been victims of this violence disproportionately...." The government's actions are manifestly insufficient because the perpetrators of this violence can continue to attack Christians and other Nigerians with impunity," said Illia Djadi, Open Doors' senior analyst on freedom of religion and belief in sub-Saharan Africa.

Other concerns.

Human rights defenders and journalists face a constant threat of intimidation and harassment. Several human rights activists and journalists have been intimidated and mistreated by police and security personnel, and some have been killed under mysterious circumstances in recent years. The benefit of freedom of expression in Nigeria is currently inadequately protected by the country's legal framework.

Abuses against women are widespread and include domestic violence, rape and other forms of sexual violence by both public officials and individuals, among other things. The authorities do not regularly exercise due diligence in preventing and responding to sexual assaults perpetrated by State and non-State actors, resulting in a culture of impunity that has taken root.

Children are often incarcerated alongside adults in police stations and prisons across the country. The only functioning pre-trial detention centre in Nigeria is overcrowded, with some 600 children housed in facilities built to house 200 young people. Given that there are more than one million street children across the country, government assistance for homeless and vulnerable children is woefully insufficient.

Attacks in Nigeria rarely appear in mainstream media, but they do appear in Christian-sponsored newspapers such as the Christian Post and the Christian Herald.

That is why extremist Islamic groups such as Boko Haram, the Islamic State of West Africa (ISWAP) and Fulani jihadists do not receive the attention they need to raise awareness. To further compound the problem, when these events are recorded, both sides are held equally responsible, attributing the cause to things like global warming, local disputes, or sectarian religious battles.

"By his grace we all unite our hearts, we will not denounce Christ. For us to live is Christ, but to die is a gain." - Amina

And the clock keeps ticking, ticking, ticking...

Iran

CHAPTER 9

IRAN

"If you are insulted because of the name of Christ, you are blessed, for the Spirit of glory and god rests upon you." 1 Peter 4:14

*****

Ayatollah Khomeini's Islamic revolution in 1979 gave rise to the world's first Shia Islamic theocracy and fundamentally altered Iran's way of life. Many Iranian citizens who once devoted their lives to Islam and Islamic rule are today filled with a sense of hopelessness and despair in a fundamentalist regime. Therefore, the Gospel is spreading throughout Iran through the Christian media and the courageous evangelists of the domestic church groupsthat are emerging In Iran.

The government's efforts to obstruct Christ's plan continue. Pastors and other Christian leaders are frequently arrested, tortured, imprisoned, and their families are tormented because of their religion. For example, apostates of Islam in Iran can be punished under Article 220 of the Iranian Penal Code and Article

167 of the Iranian Constitution. In addition, they can be subjected to the death penalty, which is known to occur under Sharia. Needless to say, some people have no choice but to flee the nation.

According to human rights organizations, the Islamic Republic of Iran is launching a massive crackdown on Christians, especially those who have converted from Islam to Christianity. Consequently, Christian converts of Muslim origin suffer the most persecution, mainly from the government and their families and communities.

Christians are being arrested and imprisoned across Iran on ambiguous charges such as support for Zionism, moharebeh – spreading corruption on Earth – anti-state propaganda, anti-Islam propaganda, deviant psychological manipulation and action against national security. In a statement, Open Doors noted that Iranian authorities frequently use a specific charge — acting against national security — "to persecute Christians for their activities in house churches."

According to Iranian leaders, the peaceful religious practices of a minority population constitute a serious threat to national security. This statement cannot be accepted under any circumstances. According to various estimates, Iran has approximately 80 million inhabitants, of which Christians represent between 117,000 and 3 million. Although Christianity constitutes a minuscule population, Christians have always been considered a threat to national security under Iranian Islamic law.

Although the Iranian government claims that more than 97% of the population is Muslim, the truth is that an uncalculated segment of the population has abandoned Islam, and many of these individuals have converted to Christ.

Government-sponsored persecution.

Christians are persecuted by the government, which has a network of informants in each city and uses them to carry out its mission of religious suppression. Christians are often persecuted by their relatives, friends, and community members, especially when knowledge of conversion is made public. In addition, Christian families are habitually dehumanized and humiliated in the community because of their participation in the Christian fellowship. It is claimed that the agents have treated Christians inhumanely.

Underground churches are frequently raided, and their leaders and members have been arrested and sentenced to long prison terms for crimes against national security, according to the FBI. In addition, the possession, printing, import and distribution of Bibles are prohibited activities. Consequently, given the difficulty Iranian believers have in obtaining a Bible, they appreciate the word of God.

According to propaganda pushed by iranian authorities, Islamists are converting to Christianity as part of a campaign by Western countries to undermine Iran's Islamic regime. As a consequence of their perception of the threat posed by Christianity, the Iranian Ministry of Intelligence Services (MOIS) and the Islamic Revolutionary Guard Corps (IRGC) monitor the activities of Christians in the Islamic Republic.

JOE IRIZARRY

Christians and other religious minorities are severely restricted from sharing their religious beliefs with others or holding religious services in Farsi, Iran's official language. The Iranian government has tried to crack down on the use of Farsi in recognized churches since 2009 and has forced the closure of churches that held services for Farsi-speaking Christians. In addition, churches are not allowed to have information about their congregation printed in Farsi. The strategy aims to make it harder for Muslim Iranians to get to know Christianity better and ultimately convert.

Visiting a house-church or a religious conference in Iran can be considered a crime. Iranian officials also consider receiving an education outside the country to be another red flag. These elements are seen as potential dangers to national security. Christians who open their doors to curious Muslims, actively proselytize, or hold a religious conversation in Farsi are automatically considered suspicious by the authorities. The most frequent charges against Christians involved in these activities are cooperation against national security, propaganda against the state, and the promotion of Zionist Christianity.

Many Iranians identify as nominal Muslims, so some new Christians find acceptance in their families and communities. Converts from more conservative Muslim families suffer tremendous persecution in their country.

Under international law, the Iranian government is obliged to safeguard the religious freedom of its citizens. Despite the fact that Christians in Iran are increasingly persecuted, and their rights are violated without precedent, the world community has kept a deafening silence about it.

According to Open Doors' most recent annual assessment, of the 50 nations in which Christians are most oppressed for their faith in Jesus, Iran is among the ten worst places to be a Christian.

Iranian followers of Christ.

One of Iran's Christian converts has begun serving a ten-month prison sentence for anti-state propaganda.

During a regular visit to his home in Fardis, located west of the Iranian capital Tehran, Hamed Ashouri, who was 31 at the time, was apprehended and detained in February 2019. Agents raided his residence and seized all items related to Christians, including Bibles and Christian literature, as well as computer hard drives and other electronic equipment. During his interrogation, Ashouri was offered a monetary reward for providing information about other Christian groups. He refused and was beaten for it.

COVID caused a delay in Ashouri's case. To secure his release, the court required him and another member of his family to attend "re-education" classes with an Islamic preacher in the form of payroll guarantees. Finally, after four sessions, Ashouri refused to appear for any more.

In preparation for his surrender to Karaj Central Prison on July 27, 2020, Ashouri filmed a short video revealing that he had been arrested for engaging in Christian activities. *"I thank God for considering me worthy to endure this persecution by Him,"* he said gratefully.

Ashouri was summoned to the Karaj Revolutionary Court on March 7, 2021 to face his original charges. On 12 April he was sentenced to ten months in prison, ten of them in solitary confinement, and on 26 June his appeal was denied.

Several human rights groups have claimed that the government has continued to harass and torture Christians who have converted from Islam. According to Voice of America (VOA), Fatemeh (Mary) Mohammadi was detained on charges of "activity against the nation security" and "advocacy against the system." After her arrest, at the Vozara Detention Centre, she was imprisoned for 24 hours without food and subjected to a naked search by the employees of the detention centre. On January 12, 2021, she received a severe beating from prison officials, both male and female, and had visible bruises for three weeks. Bail was set at about 95 million rials ($2,300) for Mohammadi, which is more than the average annual salary of an Iranian. In an April 21, 2021 Instagram post, Mohammadi revealed that she was detained for 46 days in "horrific conditions."

On July 1, 2022, nine Christians from Iran who were believed to be converts were convicted by an Islamic court and sentenced to five years in prison. They were detained by the IRGC after attending religious services at a private residence.

The following information was reported by Article 18, an Iranian non-governmental organization that advocates for religious freedom: A coordinated operation began around 9 a.m., when the officials who detained them identified themselves as agents of the Ministry of Intelligence (MOIS) and broke into the homes of Christians and confiscated Bibles, Christian literature, wooden crosses and paintings with Christian symbols, as well as laptops and telephones, as well as all kinds of identity documents, bank cards and other personal belongings.

In November 2020, intelligence agents raided several homes of converts to gather information. Mobile phones, computers and Bibles were seized; however, no one was arrested because of the raid. Earlier this year, believers were threatened with long prison sentences and were informed that it would be best to leave the country. When asked to promise to stop participating in other Christian activities, they all refused to do so.

According to Release International, which helps persecuted Christians around the world, Iran has long been a source of concern. *"Time and again, we see persecution increasing where Islamist radicals tighten their grip on power,"* said Paul Robinson, CEO of Release.

The governments of Iran, Pakistan and Nigeria have accepted (in whole or in part) sharia (Islamic law). Unfortunately, persecution as a consequence of this fundamentalism has been an inevitable result of theocratic Islamist government that has refused to compromise.

Politics and religion are inextricably intertwined in Islamic Sharia thought. And, as Iran's stance has become increasingly harsh, the Church has become embroiled in repression and is regarded as a political opponent in the country.

As described above, individuals who identify as Christians have frequently been accused of undermining national security and have found themselves in the role of adversaries of the state. In addition, religious activity that takes place outside the jurisdiction of the State is considered an attempt to destabilize the Islamic Republic.

COVID has become a weapon.

Although Armenian and Assyrian Christians are recognized and protected by the state, they are nevertheless considered second-class citizens in the eyes of the public. They cannot share their faith with others during religious services or talk about religious topics in the Persian language.

Although the Iranian authorities have maintained their level of repression, there has been a slight increase in the number of reported acts of violence. COVID has hurt the nation, and many Christians are in dire need of food and assistance. Actions to combat the virus have also made communication between Christians difficult. Consequently, more and more Christians are turning to the Internet for fraternization and discipleship.

Many Iranian prisoners, including some who were imprisoned for their religious beliefs, were released to curb the development of COVID in overcrowded prisons. Although some Christians were released, many others remained in prison. In addition, the sentences of the newly detained Christians continued.

Churches and people of Muslim origin are more vulnerable to persecution from the government and their communities. On the other hand, Christians in metropolitan areas have more freedom to organize meetings and activities than in rural areas, where social surveillance is severe.

Christianity in Iran.

"...Iran's Intelligence Minister Mahmoud Alavi openly admitted to calling Christian converts for questioning, saying mass conversions "are happening under our eyes," according to Open Door, one of the organizations that contributed to the UN Human Rights Council report. In addition, Alavi stated that his organization and Muslim seminaries work together as liaisons to prevent the "threat" of mass conversions to Christianity. Alavi later acknowledged that the physical threat is minimal. "These converts are ordinary people, whose jobs are to sell sandwiches or the like."

The Voice of the Martyrs (VOM), a renowned advocacy group, which monitors targeted violence around the world, including Iran, claims that there are currently more than a million Christians in the country, despite the country's resistance to their beliefs.

As Todd Nettleton, representative of VOM USA, explained to Worthy News on June 24, 2021, the growing number of Christians is the result of "people having seen the true face of Islam." He claimed that many Muslims convert to the Christian faith because they "do not want" to be subject to the strict restrictions of Islam.

According to one analyst, the hardline supreme leader, Ayatollah Ali Kahmenei, appointed President Raisi in response to the rise of Christianity, and he is considered the successor appointed by Kahmenei.

Independent election observers questioned his candidacy, as Muslim reformers and moderates were prohibited from running for office, which was a source of controversy.

According to estimates, only about fifty percent of the country's eligible voters voted in the June elections. The Voice of the Martyrs of Canada (VOMC) said there had been situations where Iranian citizens tried to vote but were met with physical resistance.

Christians have expressed concern about the rise in violence under Iran's new president. As the former head of the judiciary, he was accused of being complicit in the imprisonment of political dissidents. According to human rights investigators, he was a member of a "killing committee" that ordered the execution of up to 5,000 political detainees. Amnesty International, a human rights organization, has called for an investigation into the new president for crimes against humanity.

Due to Christian beliefs and cultural/ethnic identification, millions of people are subjected to interrogation, imprisonment, torture and even death.

And the clock keeps ticking, ticking, ticking...

CHAPTER 10

PAKISTAN

"But even if you suffer for what is just, you are blissful. Do not fear their threats; do not be afraid." 1 Peter 3:14

*****

In its most recent study of religious persecutors, the World Open Door Watch leader called Pakistan the fifth-worst violator of religious freedom of the fifty countries included in the analysis. In addition, in a 2021 annual report, the U.S. Commission on International Religious Freedom (USCIRF) has on more than one occasion called Pakistan a *"country of particular concern."* The Commission's recommendations include imposing sanctions and improving the security of religious communities at risk.

According to Human Rights Watch, *"law enforcement carries out arbitrary arrests and extrajudicial executions with impunity."* It is common to witness blasphemy-related violence against religious minorities, fuelled in part by government persecution and discriminatory legislation. To draw attention to these atrocities, silent protesters gathered in front of the United Nations headquarters in Geneva on June 21, 2020 to "raise their voices in solidarity to remove the malicious blasphemy law and forced conversions in Pakistan."

Forced religious conversions.

Coercive conversions are practiced against Pakistani Christians and other religious minorities, including Shia Muslims and Hindus. In most cases, forced conversions occur in bonded labour contexts or, more typically, in abductions of young women who are often raped and forced to marry their abductor. According to the Pakistani NGO Aurat Foundation, every year about 1,000 women convert to Islam by force. As indicated in your report, forced conversion is defined as any individual or persons who use coercion, pressure, force, stress or threat, whether physical, emotional or psychological, to force another person to accept another religion. It is typical for these methods to be used not only with the victim himself, but may also be used or threatened with the victim's family, loved ones, or community members.

Local officials are often complicit in these situations, as they do not conduct a thorough investigation or properly prosecute them. If they do, they often question the girl in front of the man she has been forced to marry. This situation is a problem that exists throughout the country.

Most of the time, the authorities turn a blind eye and are usually unwilling to help victims at all.

For example, when Chashman Masih, 14, did not return home from school on July 27, 2021, her father, Gulzar Masih, went to her school to pick her up. He was dismayed to discover that he had disappeared without a trace. He immediately contacted his family, who lived in the area, but did not see her that day. He later reported his daughter missing to the samnaabbad police in Faisalabad.

Gulzar, a rickshaw driver by profession, returned to the police station frequently in search of answers, but was unsuccessful. A few days later, the kidnapper sent the family a video and documentation, including a marriage certificate, an affidavit and a conversion letter to Islam, in which Chashman claimed he had converted to the religion of his own free will.

The incident had a major impact after Faisalabad human rights activist Lala Robin Daniel became involved in the investigation. His words: *"The Punjab authorities must do their job to release the abducted girls."* Daniel demanded that the kidnappers be held accountable by legal means. *"As long as the abductions continue undisturbed, the girls and their families will feel unsafe."*

In a letter published by Muhammad Ijaz Qadri, district president of the Sunni Tehreek Organization of Pakistan, Chashman's conversion to Islam was "certified," and his "Islamic name from now on will be Aisha Bibi." The Sunni Tehreek Organization supports the Barelvi Revivalist Movement, which aims to maintain Islam in the Indian subcontinent and has the support of 60% of Pakistani Muslims.

Unfortunately, what has happened to her is all too common in Pakistan; the vast majority of victims and their families confirm that Pakistani officials systematically refuse to provide any assistance to victims. Under Pakistani law, anyone who has sex with a girl under the age of 16 can be sentenced to death; however, if the girl is Muslim, once she reaches puberty, she can consent to the marriage.

Kidnapping and rape.

Venus Bibi, 30, a Christian and mother of five from Sahoo Ki Malian (village) in Sheikhupura, went to buy household items on April 1, 2021. As she returned home, random men grabbed her by the arm and took her to a nearby car before she had a chance to understand what they were saying. They insisted that I accompany them and not make a scene. Once she realized what was happening, Bibi ignored them, struggled and started screaming, but the kidnappers pulled out a revolver and threatened to shoot her if she didn't cooperate. She was frightened, stopped screaming, and obeyed. She claimed that one of her kidnappers told her that she would be taken to Sahiwal, another city located 129 kilometers (more than 80 miles) from her hometown, so that no one could discover her.

Bibi's husband, Warris Masih, said that although he had reported his wife's abduction to the police, the police did not take much action and assured him not to worry, as they were trying to locate his wife.

Bibi was held hostage for 20 days, during which she was raped and repeatedly beaten by the alleged perpetrator and his friends. The assailant and her friends threatened to kill her children and husband if she tried to flee.

Muhamad Akbar was later identified as the alleged main perpetrator of Bibi's abduction, with the help of his colleagues. Once Masih informed the authorities that Akbar was detaining his wife, they pressured Akbar to release Bibi.

Soon after, Bibi was found on the shoulder of the road, near her village, Sahoo Ki Malian, in a dreadful state, unable to move on her own. It is believed that she was only released from the custody of her kidnapper after a police case was brought against him.

Masih sobbed, explaining that because his family was poor and Christian, the police did not take action against the kidnapper. He claimed that Akbar had bribed the authorities considerably. Bibi was sitting with her head down near her husband, covering her face with a handkerchief, crying incessantly, and raising her head only to say that the kidnappers had injected her with narcotics to make sure she didn't escape.

According to Bibi and Masih, it was not the first time Akbar had kidnapped a Christian girl; he had supposedly done so in the past as well. As Akbar is wealthy and influential, the authorities never took any criminal action against him. As a result of the lack of criminal punishment, he gained confidence and continued to perpetrate these acts regularly. *"But I want justice for my wife. I want all the kidnappers to be arrested and punished for their crimes so that they stop kidnapping more Christian women,"* Masih said.

As AsiaNews reported, on June 6, 2021, Danish Masih, a 17-year-old Christian boy from Ghafari, disappeared; two days later, his father, Daniyal, reported his son missing, but police made no effort to locate him. Masih was reportedly drugged and knocked unconscious before being kidnapped by a Muslim named Ali Raza and his friends. He was kidnapped, tortured and raped in an unknown location for five days before leaving him near Faisalabad, a desolate region of the country. Eventually, the victim was able to return home on his own.

The father, Daniyal, decided to ask human rights activist Lala Robin Daniel for help, who spoke to AsiaNews about the situation. Daniel expressed his dissatisfaction with the police's stance: *"As Christians, we are a minority and we are alone. For us there is no justice or equal rights."*

No one has been arrested, although authorities say they are actively searching for the perpetrators. Masih's family, for their part, is demanding restitution.

Masih's story is not an isolated case. In Pakistan, violence against Christians is all too frequent. Faced with rising violence figures, the Catholic Justice and Peace Commission organized a seminar in Sahiwal's Sacred Heart Parish to call on the federal and provincial legislatures to pass new laws to end these practices.

Christians in the spotlight.

The Christians of Pakistan suffer severe persecution in virtually every aspect of their existence. In this predominantly Islamic country, believers who have converted to Islam suffer the most severe degrees of persecution, but all Christians are treated as second-class citizens. They are usually assigned jobs considered low-paid, dirty and disreputable, and may be victims of bonded labour. Although some Christians belong to the middle class, they are often considered inferior to their Muslim counterparts and are often subject to severe employment discrimination.

Pakistan's Christian communities are the target of the famous blasphemy laws, which Islamic extremist groups vigorously "uphold," even attacking and killing people deemed to have violated the provisions of the laws.

After receiving a text message on WhatsApp, a Christian woman from Pakistan was arrested and charged with allegedly violating the country's strict blasphemy laws. After the arrest, the Christian woman's family was forced to flee their home because she received death threats from religious fanatics.

As first reported by International Christian Concern, Shagufta Rafiq was arrested on 29 July 2021 in Islamabad after being accused of committing blasphemy and taken into custody during an armed police raid on her residence. Rafiq was charged under Sections 295-A and 295-B of Pakistan's blasphemy law, and if convicted, she can be sentenced to life imprisonment.

Shagufta Rafiq's husband, Rafiq Masih, told the International Criminal Court that numerous police officers and law enforcement representatives broke into his home on 29 July. *"They harassed my family and took our phones, laptops and other valuables,"* Masih said. *"The police were fully armed and ordered us not to move and keep our hands up. They detained*

Shagufta, my two sons and my daughter without any prior information or arrest warrant."

According to Rafiq, the arrest came in the wake of his participation in a WhatsApp discussion group in which a member had uploaded an allegedly blasphemous message. Rafiq was accused of committing blasphemy against Islam, although she was not the author of the message.

According to Masih, Rafiq had no knowledge of the message, although she was accused of having passed it on to others. Shagufta has categorically denied these allegations.

In Pakistan, blasphemy is a punishable "crime" that can sometimes lead to the death penalty.

Some progress.

Although the persecution continues, there have been some beneficial advances.

Forced religious conversions are now illegal in Pakistan's Sindh province, which enacted a law on November 24, 2016, known as the Criminal Law (Protection of Minorities) Act of 2015. In December 2015, Nand Kumar Goklani, a member of the Sindh provincial assembly who belongs to the Hindu minority community and the Pakistan Muslim League political party, introduced a private bill.

The same provincial assembly passed a law creating the Sindh Minority Rights Commission, which aims to *"provide a platform to examine the grievances of minority communities, suggest mechanisms to accelerate the pace of their socio-economic development, and promote and protect their identities at the provincial level."*

The Sindh administration has also been threatened by protests from religious and political parties opposing these new laws. Several multiparty conferences were held to criticize the new law just one month after its passage. The main argument used by the opposition *"claimed that the new law went against the teachings of Islam, the Constitution of Pakistan and the Charter of the United Nations..."*

Although progress has been made in Pakistan's Sindh province, forced conversion across the country remains legal in most other parts of the country.

Additional legislative changes are being made to some local laws to limit certain discriminatory information directed at religious minorities. Starting in 2021, the government created a unified national curriculum that will be applied in all schools, including the approximately 35,000 madrassas that currently exist. In part, these measures can be attributed to diplomatic pressure exerted by the United States, which included a visit by U.S. Ambassador General for International Religious Freedom Samuel Brownback in February 2019.

Recently, the death penalty has been avoided in several high-profile blasphemy cases in which the defendants faced an execution sentence.

Although Christian churches exist, those engaged in outreach continue to be subject to tremendous discrimination and persecution by society.

And the clock keeps ticking, ticking, ticking...

Libya

CHAPTER 11

LIBYA

"When you are persecuted in one place, flee to another. Truly, I say to you, you will not finish touring the cities of Israel before the Son of Man comes." Matthew 10:23

*****

Libya is a country with two internal governments in conflict, each backed by a different regional foreign power. According to the United Nations, Turkey supports the internationally recognized Government of National Accord (GNA), while Egypt supports the Libyan National Army (LNA), which opposes it.

Historically, an overwhelming number of nations around the world have recognized Turkey's genocide against Armenian Christians, which occurred a century ago. Turkey has remained steadfast in its general denial of genocide, despite the overwhelming international and historical consensus against it. The Libyan National Army issued a statement of recognition of the

Armenian genocide in response to Turkey's increased military involvement in Libya.

While Libya and Turkey debate the previous genocide, Egypt reminds Turkey of history with the Ottoman Empire. The two countries are increasingly at odds over their support for different parties in Libya.

In 2020, Turkey made it very clear that the Libyan war was one of its main foreign policy concerns and consequently intensified its military engagement in the country.

Because of these unrest, not only has the civil conflict been complicated, but Christians in the three countries have been firmly targeted in these geopolitical maneuvers. The governments of these countries have a long history of violations of religious freedom, accusations of Islamic conquest, and genocide against Christianity. That is why Christians in Libya, Turkey and Egypt are particularly vulnerable targets.

Cristianofobia.

Libyans are predominantly Sunni Muslims, between 90 and 95% identify as such, Ibadi Muslims represent about 5% and Christians between 2 and 3% of the total population; an important part of these Christiansare expatriates and working emigrants . In Libya there are a small number of believers who rarely have the opportunity to practice their religion publicly in the country.

In Libya, life is a challenge, but the challenges are compounded for Christians, especially those who have converted from Islam to Christianity. Christianphobic attitudes are prevalent among Muslim relatives, neighbors, and friends. People who have converted can have their family or occupation taken away. In some extreme cases, they have been beaten, tortured or killed for their faith. For Christians of Muslim origin in Libya, the pressure from their family and the wider community to abandon their faith is severe and fierce. Their abduction or murder by Islamic terrorist groups, organized crime syndicates and foreign Christians are a constant threat. The number of Christians held captive in Libya is unknown, as kidnappings are frequent among the country's militias.

Since the revolution and the overthrow of Libyan dictator Tyrant Muammar Gaddafi in 2011, the country has remained unstable and chaotic. In recent years, there has been an increase in verified attacks and fatalities in Libya, which is worrying, and the violence has caused many to flee the country en masse. Many missionaries, local Christians and journalists have been killed, so outreach activities in the country and information about the atrocities have been ruthlessly suppressed.

At present, rival administrations are vying for control of the country, and the resulting conflicts have severely devastated the country's infrastructure and made sharing the Gospel in the area extremely difficult and dangerous. In addition, Bibles are severely limited throughout the country and must be brought with great difficulty and risk to be distributed. Owning a Bible, especially the digital formats used in mobile phones and laptops, is an insecure act. Unfortunately, freedom of expression, religion, women's rights and other fundamental human rights are almost non-existent in Libya.

Although Libyan law does not openly prohibit Christianity, the 2011 Libyan Constitutional Declaration restricts the public expression of one's religious beliefs, and people who attempt to share their Christian beliefs and proselytize face significant fines and even jail time. Since the country has become a chaotic anarchy due to the lack of a central administration, there is little hope of obtaining legal redress when people are attacked or killed.

Although Christians are threatened across the country, those living in places where Islamic extremist groups operate are the most vulnerable. Individuals and groups that have pledged allegiance to the Islamic State have a significant presence in the city of Sirte and the surrounding region. Many other extremist groups have taken control of the territory of Tripoli, the country's capital, and its environs.

To avoid harassment, Christians residing near Tripoli often avoid travel, especially where there may be checkpoints; however, migrants often do not have that option.

Migrants.

Christian refugees (most of them from sub-Saharan African countries and the Philippines) often try to enter Europe and use Libya as a transit country. While in transit, they are often captured by officials and detained in overcrowded detention camps at and around Tripoli airport. It is reportedly not uncommon for migrants detained in these detention centres to have been raped and beaten while in custody.

Some refugees are tricked by human traffickers, who use false promises of transport to Europe, to extort their victims to perform intensive agricultural work or engage in prostitution. Often, these traffickers subject victims to physical, psychological abuse and blackmail, especially if the victims try to escape.

Although Christian refugees are not the only ones who suffer inappropriate treatment and violence, Christians are subjected to significantly more discriminatory and violent treatment than the general population.

After CNN aired video evidence of a slave auction involving sub-Saharan Africans in Libya in November 2017, the country grabbed international attention. Despite the international outcry that followed the report's immediate release, little seems to have changed.

Martyred by Christ.

In two separate attacks that occurred (December 2014 and January 2015), the men were working as migrants in Sirte to support their family, in their home country, when they were captured by the Islamic State (ISIS). The captors looked at the workers' ID cards, freed all the Muslim captives and kept the 21 Christian men.

In February 2015, the captives were taken to a beach in Sirte wearing an orange jump suit. Each Christian man was paired with a masked jihadist in black with a knife and ordered to kneel on the edge of the shore. Several of the men were praying silently. Subsequently, the Islamic State murdered each of the Christians in a video titled *"People of the Cross, Followers of the Hostile Egyptian Church."* Local media reported that the last man, the twenty-first victim, named Matthew Ayariga, a Ghanaian Christian, was asked his religion and his answer was: *"I am a Christian, and I am like them."*

The Islamic State's reign of terror in Iraq, Syria, Egypt, Libya and Afghanistan reached infamy with the release of this film.

Although the bodies of the other 20 men were discovered and taken to their homeland in Egypt in October 2017, Ayariga's body was not recovered until 2020.

As reported on September 29, 2020 by Cairo-based journalist Farid Y. Farid, the body of Matthew Ayariga, who was beheaded along with 20 other Coptic Christians on a beach in Sirte, Libya, in a video released by the Islamic State in February 2015, has finally been buried. According to Farid, who has written for publications such as The New York Times and other *publications, "his remains have finally arrived today in Egypt to be buried, [with] his Coptic brothers, after [more than] 5 years of his body not being claimed."*

Father Abu Fanus Unan works in the Church of the Martyrs of the Faith and fatherland. He stated: *"The Coptic Church has a long history of martyrdom and has gone through many times of persecution throughout its history. We are proud of the blood of these martyrs who refused to retract their Christian faith."* Ayariga's remains have been returned to the church, where they will be buried next to their fellow martyrs.

The mother of two of the martyred Coptic Christians, Samuel (22) and Beshoy (24), called herself "mother of martyrs" and expressed with great confidence her firm conviction that they were in heaven. *"I'm proud of them,"* she told Aid to the Church in Need (AIN), which is a Catholic program that provides humanitarian assistance to persecuted Church members around the world.

Zaki Hanna, father of one of the victims, told Reuters:

"I wanted to see Milad come back from Libya with his feet on the ground after his struggle and his hard work to make a living abroad. But thank God, he died as a hero, he begged no one to spare his life and he and his brothers, the martyrs, did not abandon their faith or their homeland."

"The blood of our fellow Christians is a witness that cries out to be heard. It doesn't matter if they are Catholic, Orthodox, Coptic or Protestant. They are Christians!" Pope Francis said as he addressed the leaders of the Church of Scotland. *"His only words were, 'Jesus, help me! They were killed simply for being Christians."*

Extremist groups.

Extremist organizations, such as the Muslim Brotherhood and the self-styled Islamic State (ISIS), operate throughout the country, including the capital.

Since its founding, ISIS has used crucifixion to humiliate the dead. In their eyes, comparing Christians to Jesus Christ is a huge insult. Islamist terrorists have stated that their ultimate goal is to eliminate Christianity from all their respective regions.

In April 2015, ISIS released a video showing the murder of 28 Ethiopian Christian men; about 12 of the men were dressed in orange jump suits and were beheaded on a beach, while the other group of 16 men dressed in black were shot in the head in a bush area. The title of the video was *"cross worshippers belonging to the hostile Ethiopian church."* These men were innocent Ethiopians trying to emigrate to Europe.

The United States condemned the "brutal mass murder" and confirmed that the men were killed "solely because of their faith, exposing the ruthless and senseless brutality of the terrorists."

Locals claim that the Islamic State has been trying to coerce people into joining its military ranks to conquer and defeat the Libyan National Army. They have announced seminars titled *"The Beginning of the End"* as part of their campaign to get non-believers to join their cause. Those who refuse to swear allegiance to the group will be killed by other members.

The fourth worst place to be a Christian.

In the case of the Armenians, Greeks and Assyrians, there is no doubt that religion played a crucial role in the Armenian genocide. Ethnic identity conflict is one of the most frequently cited factors; however, while legitimate, religion has historically played as much or more important a role in defining a person's identity than their language or cultural history; in fact, it has it for the Muslim doctrine of wala wa bara or Loyalty and Enmity.

Many Muslim governments, mobs, jihadists and extremist groups persecute Christian minorities throughout the Islamic world. Although many of these people share the same ethnicity, language and culture as Muslims, they do not share religious beliefs.

Libya is ranked No. 4 on the Open Doors global watch list due to the great repression and persecution against Christians.

If we do not confront and address the horror currently suffered by millions of Christians throughout the Islamic world, which, according to the United Nations, has reached proportions of genocide in some areas, we will be complicit in it. To put it another way, those who want to commit genocide are always helped and instigated by silence.

Who today warns of the ongoing extermination of Christians under the Islamic rule of law?

And the clock keeps ticking, ticking, ticking...

Somalia

CHAPTER 12

SOMALIA.

"... persecuted, but not abandoned; beaten, but not destroyed." 2 Corinthians 4:9

*****

Somalia is a Muslim-majority country with a longhistory of religious prejudice. Although Somalia's Interim Federal Constitution does not explicitly impose limitations on the practice of religions other than Islam, the government and all laws are based on sharia; all citizens (Muslims and non-Muslims) are equally obliged to abide by its rules.

For years, there was a general sense of informal tolerance towards Somali Christians. Although they were a tiny number, Christians were allowed to worship in their respective churches freely. However, due to the increase in the Christian population, the government's tolerance began to change, and the entry of Christian missionaries into the country was restricted.

In 2006, the Union of Islamic Courts (ICU) seized authority in southern Somalia, and in 2009 sharia was officially recognized as the country's legal system.

Since then, Muslim extremists, particularly those linked to al-Shabaab, have taken control of much of Somalia and persecuted some of the last Christians for their religious views, some of whom were deported, shot dead or beheaded as a result of their personal beliefs. Among those affected are not only religious officials and men, but also women and children.

Persecutions of Christians are frequently made public to prevent other Somalis from converting to Christianity. Many groups have zero tolerance for Christianity and will do everything in their power to prevent it from spreading further.

Al-Shabaab.

The Harakat Shabaab al-Mujahidin, also known as al-Shabaab, is an extremist Islamic terrorist organization based in Somalia that is in favor of sharia (Islamic law) as a basis for governing all aspects of life and is a major threat in the country.

Al-Shabaab is an Arabic word that translates to "youth" and refers to young men who seek to impose a rigid interpretation of Islamic law on Somalia, which includes the murder of anyone who is not a Muslim. These extremists who persecute Christians pretend to satisfy Allah because they believe that Christians are enemies of God.

A major problem contributing to the spread of anti-Christian propaganda is that the majority of Somalis are illiterate. Out of 216 countries, Somalia ranks 210th in terms of literacy, with only 37.8 per cent of the population literate. Often, the uninformed population tends to rely on rumors as a source of knowledge. As a result, when people hear the indoctrination that condemns the "Western imperialist" philosophy, they are more likely to believe the stories and decide that Christianity should be abolished.

According to the Office of the Director of National Intelligence, al-Shabaab was at one point the militant wing of the Somali Council of Islamic Courts and had taken control of a significant part of southern and central Somalia in 2006. In 2007 they were defeated by the Federal Government of Somalia with the help of Ethiopian forces; however, they maintained control of certain strategic locations. They are known to recruit (voluntarily or not) members of other factions or groups to use terror and guerrilla warfare tactics against the Federal Government of Somalia, African Union Mission in Somalia peacekeepers and non-governmental aid organizations. In 2008, the United States designated al-Shabaab as a Foreign Terrorist Organization.

Violence in southern Somalia is multiplying due to the country's Civil War, which began in 2009 and is actively continuing. The civil war pits the Federal Government of Somalia against the help of African Union peacekeeping troops against multiple militant Islamist groups and factions. Islamic extremists fighting in the south often go public with persecutions of Christians to prevent other Somalis from converting to Christianity. In general, they have zero tolerance for Christian conversion. Under Sharia, proselytizing of any religion other than Islam is illegal throughout the country. In February 2012, al-Shabaab merged with al Qaeda.

Al-Shabaab has been responsible for multiple bombings, including several suicide attacks. Since 2013, they have attacked in other countries, including Kenya, in the September 2013 attack on Nairobi's Westgate shopping mall (67 victims), in the attack on a Djiboutian restaurant in May 2014 and in the Garissa University massacre in April 2015 (which killed 150 students, mainly Christian). In addition, in October 2016, al-Shabaab killed six Christians in northeastern Kenya with a grenade and gun attack. Since Kenya shares a border with Somalia, these attacks are known to occur.

Inside Somalia, al-Shabaab claimed responsibility for the killings of Somali peace activists, public figures, international aid workers and the blockade of aid during the 2011 famine, which allegedly killed thousands of Somalis.

Guled Jama Muktar, a 17-year-old Somali Christian, was beheaded in the Mogadishu area by al-Shabaab in October 2011. On 25 September, Muktar was attacked at home while his parents were working. Al-Shabaab had been watching his family since Christians arrived in Somalia from Kenya in 2008. When the parents learned of their son's murder, they buried him and fled the city.

In another incident, in January 2013, a failed attempt to rescue a French hostage in Somalia, who had been held captive for more than three years, resulted in the death of the hostage, two French commandos, 17 Islamist militants and at least two civilians.

SIGNS OF THE TIMES: *THE GREAT PERSECUTION*

According to the United Nations, Al-Shabaab has been attacking the people of Somalia at an alarming rate. They have carried out large-scale personal attacks and terrorist acts in which many people have been killed at the same time. Although the group has weakened significantly in recent years due to the African Union's ongoing military effort, it is still considered the most serious threat to Somalia's Christians.

Divorced and beaten.

When a husband discovered that his wife, a 32-year-old mother of two, had a Somali-language Bible in her hands, he demanded that he identify where he had received it. According to the Morning Star News report, it was at that moment that the woman realized she had forgotten to close the drawer where she kept her precious Bible. Although she secretly converted to Christianity in 2016, she told her husband that she had found the book and wanted to read it.

"He just uttered the word talaq [divorce] for me. I knew that our marriage had just been annulled because I had joined Christianity, so, without wasting time, I left home," he explained. "He sternly warned me not to approach the boys (two girls aged 7 and 4), and that if I did, I would take the Bible to the Islamic court and be killed by stoning for becoming an apostate."

After her husband informed his family of his discovery, she faced punishment from her brothers. The woman told how her brothers mistreated her by beating her with sticks and refusing to feed her. "*I was afraid to report the case to the police or the local administration, because I would be charged with a crime of apostasy under Sharia.*" After her escape, the young mother moved to an unnamed city, many hours away from her home.

According to the U.S. State Department, Somalia's constitution declares Islam as the country's official religion and prohibits the spread of any other faith. It also requires that laws be based on sharia principles, with no exceptions for non-Muslims.

"God has spared my life, and my fellow underground Christians from other regions of Somalia have welcomed me and shared what little they have, but I am very traumatized."

On the verge of eradication.

According to the Open Door Global Watch List, Somalia ranks third in the world for persecution of Christians, behind Afghanistan and North Korea. The fight against the significant oppression suffered by Christians in Somalia is one of the most important challenges in the world.

Today, it is estimated that there are fewer than a thousand Christians among Somalia's 15 million people; this constitutes less than 0.01% of the population. Most of these Christians live in the southern regions of Somalia, where the risk to the remaining Christians is most severe, as a significant part of the fighting occurs in that area.

Islam is a vital component of Somali identity, and any Somali accused of converting to Christianity may face grave danger. Many times, Christians and converts are forced to hide their faith from society in order to blend in with the Islamic majority. If their conversion is discovered, Christian women may be raped and/or married against their will. If a Christian man is killed or kidnapped, the family suffers because he is usually the breadwinner. Other family members are often left unprotected and considered a social scourge.

On his way home from work in December 2013, two individuals shot and killed Abdikhani Hassan, a married man with a pregnant wife and five children, accusing him of proselytizing (spreading his faith).

As you can imagine, it is almost impossible to publicly declare Christian beliefs in Somalia, as doing so can carry a high cost of harassment, intimidation or even death at the hands of relatives, clans or the community.

There are no active ecclesiastical buildings in the whole country. Mogadishu's cathedral suffered damage in the 1980s and was due to be repaired in 2013; however, construction never began.

Government oversight.

In addition, Somali Christians cannot practice their religion because they are forced to follow Muslim customs. In 2015, Somalia banned the celebration of holidays such as Christmas and New Year's. According to a Reuters interview with Mogadishu Mayor Abdifatah Halane's spokesman, "Christmas will not be celebrated in Somalia for two reasons: all Somalis are Muslims and there is no Christian community here. The other reason is for safety... Christmas is for Christians. Not for Muslims." According to the government, Christians can continue to celebrate the holiday, but only in private. Observing the party openly and excessively is punishable by up to five years in prison.

Al-Shabaab banned school bells in some cities because they rang too much like church bells, which was insulting. In addition, Al-Shabaab terrorists beheaded Sadia Ali Omar, 41, and Osma Mohamoud, her 35-year-old cousin, in March 2014, after they declared their intention to "wipe out any underground Christians" living in their region. The Islamists forced Omar's two daughters (8 and 15 years old) to watch helplessly, unable to save their mother.

Because of the likelihood of being killed if they try to defend Christianity in Somalia, Somali Christians have no representation in any branch of government that can provide them with security.

These limitations pose a challenge for Somali Christians, both culturally and socially. They have to meet in secret because they fear being detected and potentially killed if they are discovered. They are also frequently forced to act muslimly following Islamic social conventions and rituals. For example, fasting from dawn to dusk during the month of Ramadan and the slaughter of lambs or goats are some of these practices.

For most of their lives, Somali men and women are separated in traditional Islamic society, and women choose to stay at home with their children while men go to work. This situation is especially difficult for women because they have little control over their circumstances.

Although the Bible requires Christians to spread the Gospel to others, the country's small Christian community cannot do so in Somalia. This denial of religious freedom is a flagrant violation of Article 18 of the Universal Declaration of Human Rights, which states:

"Everyone has the right to freedom of thought, conscience and religion; this right includes the freedom to change one's religion or belief, as well as the freedom to manifest one's religion or belief, individually and collectively, both in public and in private, by teaching, practice, worship and observance."

Kenya, Somalia's neighbour, is seeing an increase in the number of Somali Christians seeking asylum. Kenya has a high Christian population and Christianity is the most widely practiced religion in the country. The number of Christian refugees arriving in Nairobi, Kenya's capital, is growing by the hundreds each year.

According to the U.S. Refugee Settlement Office, in addition to administering aid, the United States has taken in some 90,000 Somali refugees between 2001 and 2015.

And the clock keeps ticking, ticking, ticking...

CHAPTER 13

NORTH KOREA

"That is why, out of love for Christ, I delight in weaknesses, in insults, in hardships, in persecutions, in difficulties. Because when I am weak, then I am strong." 2 Corinthians 12:10

*****

In an August 2021 report by the Korea Future Initiative, a non-governmental organization that investigates human rights violations, North Korea's communist dictatorship has used its regime to commit improper detentions, torture – including deprivation of food, water and sleep – sexual violence, executions and the denial of fundamental religious freedom rights as part of its campaign to "exterminate all adherents and institutions". Christians."

According to the report by the U.S. Commission on International Religious Freedom, titled "Organized Persecution – Documentation of Religious Freedom Violations in North Korea," it refers to "these violations, which have been documented to occur through 2020, are apparently designed to eliminate all traces of Christianity..."

North Korea has a Ministry of State Security which is a government organization that is a counterintelligence office, composed of officials and informants in both North Korea and China. One of its responsibilities is to keep religion out of the country and to exterminate all Christian adherents; they are considered to be "brutally effective" through their use of "dead-end" political prison and labor camps.

The North Korean governmental structure also discourages most religion through an educational (i.e., schools) and organizational (i.e., workplaces) system that strongly discourage religious practice or adherence, especially Christianity. Members of that system are so indoctrinated, that it is common and expected for neighbors, co-workers, and even friends or family members to report someone for practicing Christianity. If they do not report the events witnessed, and the informants or the government learn of their dissonance, they too can and will often be punished as severely as the practicing individual. People who worship Christ may not be the only individuals who pay the price, as the entire family (up to four generations) may also face punishment due to one person's decision.

The freedoms of North Korean citizens are subject to and restricted by a document titled "Ten Principles for the Establishment of a Monolithic Ideological System," which purports that the thoughts and actions of each individual conform to the teachings of leaders Kim Il-Sung, Kim Jong-il and Kim Jong-un, who command total and absolute loyalty. All citizens must memorize the document, which includes ten fundamental principles and sixty-five clauses.

Although North Korea claims that its country allows freedom of religion, it does not, as Christians are a target. According to United Nations reports, the total number of Christians in the country is estimated to range from 200,000 to 400,000, although the actual figure is impossible to calculate at this time.

In 2014, the group Aid to the Church in Need claimed that approximately 50,000 Christians were in North Korean detention camps. In addition, "since 1953, at least 200,000 Christians have disappeared. If captured by the regime, unauthorized Christians face torture or, in some cases, public execution."

North Korea's History with Christianity.

In 1910, the Treaty of Annexation was signed between Japan and Korea, and the Korean peninsula became part of the Japanese Empire. At this time, pro-American sentiment and Christianity began to grow in popularity due to Korean nationalist opposition to Japanese rule.

After World War II, the Japanese Empire lost control of most of its territories, including the Korean Peninsula. In 1945, the Soviets (and communist influence) took control of the north, while the United States (with democratic influence) took control of the southern part of the country.

There were said to be 500,000 Christians in North Korea in 1945, when the Korean peninsula was divided; among them was a devout Christian family: Kang Ban Sok, an elder of a Christian church who established an anti-Japanese women's society, and Kim Hyong Jik, a Korean patriot who fought against the Japanese Empire. Kim Song-Ju was born to the couple on April 15, 1912. Later, this boy would join a Russian communist youth organization and be renamed Kim Il-Sung. He would lead the country as prime minister and president before becoming North Korea's first president in 1972.

Kim Il-Sung knew his family's devotion to Christianity and God, and envied that same loyalty and power. He proclaimed the day of his birth as a divine point in history, emulating the meaning of Jesus in the Western calendar. This three-day holiday is called "The Day of the Sun". Moreover, in North Korea, his words became law, worship or praise in a process of near-deification. A new religion, Junche (self-sufficiency), was created to worship the Kim family. Individuals who failed to comply were often punished harshly, including labor camps or death. This same brutal and arrogant personality was passed on to his son, Kim Jong-il, and his grandson, current leader Kim Jong-un.

The goal of eradicating Christianity.

A report by the U.S. Commission on International Religious Freedom confirms how far the North Korean regime is willing to go to eradicate any trace of Christian belief in the country. *"Our findings establish that the persecution of people exercising their right to religious freedom in North Korea goes far beyond a government that neglects its duty to respect, protect and fulfil the right to freedom of thought, conscience, religion or belief."*

Individuals who are caught practicing religion or simply suspected of possessing religious items in private are liable to punishment. Proselytizing is impossible in North Korea, as the possession and distribution of religious texts remains a criminal offense under the law. Even finding a few pages of the Bible can mean immediate death or imprisonment in one of the terrible prisons or labor camps where slavery, torture, deprivation, and death are common.

According to the Open Door World Watch List, North Korea is the second most dangerous country in the world to be a Christian. It is estimated that there are some 50,000 Christian believers held captive in terrible prisons and labor camps, of which only a small percentage are released. We appreciate this study, which is an important contribution to attempts to draw international attention to the plight of our persecuted family in North Korea.

Cruel treatment and abuse.

Between 1990 and 2019, the Korea Future Initiative conducted 384 interviews with survivors, witnesses and perpetrators of religious persecution in North Korea, all of whom had defected from the country. The interviews covered a wide range of topics related to religious persecution. A total of 91 Christians have been recognized as victims, ranging in age from a baby to individuals in their eighties.

The Korea Future Initiative has also identified various forms of torture that the government applies against its people, including being forced to hang on steel bars while being beaten with a wooden stick; being hung by the legs; having their bodies tightly tied with sticks; being forced to perform "squat jumps" and to sit and get up hundreds or thousands of times each day; having a liquid made with red pepper powder. forcibly poured into their nostrils; be forced to kneel with a wooden bar inserted between the knee shafts; strangulation; be forced to witness the execution or torture of other prisoners; hunger; be forced to eat contaminated food; be forced to be in isolation; be sleep deprived; and be forced to remain seated and motionless at the mast and more than 12 hours a day.

According to the U.S. Commission on International Religious Freedom, "In March 2022, three members of the Lee Min Park family were arrested in a joint raid by agents of the Central Command of the Ministry of State Security and the Ministry of State Security of South Hwanghae, after four months of surveillance and wiretapping. After 30 days of pre-trial interrogation, they were sentenced to execution for practicing Christian worship." In another incident, six people were convicted of practicing Christianity and subsequently executed by firing squad in 2015. Another 40 people were sentenced to life in prison in a political prison camp.

Supposedly, an unidentified Christian convert was imprisoned in a metal cage only 1 meter by 1 meter wide, with electrified bars. Although most convicts can serve a maximum sentence of three or four hours, their prayer earned him an excessive punishment of 12 hours in the cage. The man got dirty and fainted, and although he was unconscious, he was taken out of the cage and beaten by the guards, causing significant injuries to his face and right leg.

Women in labor camps, especially pregnant women, can be subjected to horror. At any time, they can be injected with medications to induce labor. After giving birth, women can be separated from their baby, who will then be suffocated by guards with plastic sheets or cloth bags and thrown in the trash.

According to one witness, a five-person firing squad is known to execute convicts strapped to a wooden stake, for a simple infraction such as possession of a Bible. In addition, a member of the Workers' Party of Korea was arrested for possessing a Bible and was executed at Hyesan airfield in front of 3,000 civilians.

Given the severity of the persecution against Christians, it is miraculous that the underground church in North Korea has not only survived, but is thriving and growing. One Christian shared with Open Doors USA his hope that *"one day the borders will open and they will be able to join forces with the South Korean and Chinese churches to preach the Gospel in some of the most isolated regions of the face of the planet."*

No one can deny that Christians in North Korea are subjected to one of the most severe regimes of persecution on the planet in terms of religious freedom. Until 2022, they were ranked by Open Doors USA as the country with the most severe persecution of Christians for twenty consecutive years.

Freedom of religion.

Although the North Korean constitution guarantees "freedom of religious belief," the regime has maintained its crackdown on the religious activities of unregistered religious organizations. Religious freedom in the country is virtually non-existent: the country is officially an atheist state and government policy continues to interfere with people's ability to practice a religion.

According to the U.S. Commission on International Religious Freedom, Shin Nam Ki recalled the propaganda with which North Korea influences its population. "When I was little I thought that almost all missionaries were Americans. However, as I got older, I started to know better." Apart from the curricular contents, this perspective was fostered through graphic novels rather than films. They were graphic novels with content such as Christian missionaries inducing children into a church and drawing blood from them in basements. These comics were published by the government."

United Nations Secretary-General Antonio Guterres said COVID-19 restrictions "have allowed the government to further suppress the flow of information and ideas among its people." As a result of COVID, the country has even more restricted freedom of movement and repression of rights.

Approximately 150,000 to 200,000 people are actively detained in internment camps. The number of

Christians currently imprisoned in these labor camps is estimated to be in the tens of thousands. Families of believers are tried guilty by association and may also be sent to labor camps or prisons. In concentration camps, life is horrible. Believers are often whipped with metal rods and forced to work 12 hours a day. They will almost certainly be shot or tortured if they try to flee. Many will suffer post-traumatic stress for the rest of their lives, even if they survive.

The religious acts that are punished are the preaching of religion, the possession of religious items, prayer, the singing of hymns and interaction with religious persons. Despite the danger, North Korean Christians believe it is worth risking for Jesus, and they keep asking for more Bibles.

And the clock keeps ticking, ticking, ticking...

CHAPTER 14

AFGHANISTAN.

"Dear friends, do not be surprised at the trial by fire that has come upon you to test you, as if something strange were happening to you. On the contrary, rejoice because you participate in the sufferings of Christ, so that you may rejoice when his glory is manifested. If you are insulted because of the name of Christ, you are blessed, for the Spirit of glory and god rests upon you."
1 Peter 4:12-14

*****

The persecution of Christians is quite severe in Afghanistan, and all Christians are in danger. Taliban-controlled areas are exceptionally oppressive, and there is no safe place in Afghanistan to practice any form of Christianity.

The Christians of Afghanistan have predominantly converted from Islam; however, according to Islamic law, apostasy is an hudood crime. Hudood crimes are crimes that go against Islamic law and some of them may constitute a capital crime. Because of the cultural pressures of living in a Muslim-majority nation and the prohibition of apostasy, the small Christian community has long practiced its faith in secret. Christians are known to constitute a small minority among Afghanistan's estimated 38 million inhabitants. Before Taliban control, the Christian population was estimated at between 10,000 and 20,000 people, although the current number is unknown.

In Afghanistan, renouncing Islam can be considered an indication of mental disorder, and a Christian convert can undergo psychiatric therapy. When a convert's family discovers that the new believer has become a Christian, the family, clan, or tribe must defend his "honor" by repudiating and, in extreme situations, killing him. Abandoning Islam is considered an exceptional source of humiliation, and Christian converts fear that if the authorities discover their new faith, they will face dire consequences. Many times, fleeing the country is the only option after conversion to Christianity.

The influence of the Taliban.

During the previous Taliban rule in Afghanistan, which lasted from 1996 to 2001, Christians and other religious minorities were severely oppressed. For example, under the government's rigid interpretation of "sacred" Islamic law, individuals were frequently subjected to harsh punishments such as public flogging, amputations, and executions.

As a result of U.S. involvement on the ground, Afghanistan's Christian community flourished following the removal of the Taliban-led government by coalition forces in 2001. Several Afghan Christians have even updated their religious affiliation on their national ID cards.

According to a 2019 State Department statement on religious freedom, the Taliban selectively persecuted and executed people in certain parts of the country because of their religious beliefs or ties to the Afghan government. Religious leaders faced death threats for teaching topics that contradicted the movement's rigorous and austere view of Islam.

The oppression of Christians in Afghanistan resumed after the U.S. military withdrew from the country by the Deadline of August 31, 2021. Following the U.S. withdrawal, the Taliban overthrew the U.S.-backed government in Kabul and established the Islamic Emirate of Afghanistan, raising fears in the country's Christian community that the brutality that characterized the Taliban's original rule before 2001 would be reinstated. According to the media, Taliban forces persecuted and killed Christians and other religious minorities.

Taliban control of Afghanistan has disastrous ramifications for Christians across the country. According to the CEO of Open Doors USA, David Curry, in a statement to the Daily Caller, "the free practice of religion is probably close to extinction." He continued: "The Taliban are known for their extremely strict interpretation of Sharia. Under their control, women are severely oppressed, violent attacks are common, and people who convert outside Islam are especially at risk of being tortured and killed by Taliban members."

"I'm not exaggerating to say that the Taliban are killing Christians," Nina Shea, director of the Hudson Institute's Center for Religious Freedom, said during an interview with Blaze TV host Glenn Beck in August 2021. Shea later described how a washington, D.C.-based think tank tried to help a Christian man in his attempt to evacuate Afghanistan after his brother and father were killed in the country. *"And he's hiding near the airport, waiting to get out, waiting to be rescued because he'll be next. And it's because he's a Christian."* Shea said Christians in Afghanistan are in danger because they are converting from Islam and are persecuted for abandoning their faith. Moreover, "that is considered in the eyes of the Taliban as an apostasy that must be punished with death."

According to reports from Christian broadcaster SAT-7, which broadcasts in 25 countries in the Middle East and North Africa, Taliban militants reportedly visit each home one by one and confront people in public if they are suspected of being Christians or opposed to Taliban control.

Sat-7 North America President Dr. Rex Rogers made the following statement: "We are hearing from reliable sources that the Taliban demand people's phones, and if they find a downloaded Bible on your device, they will kill you immediately... It's incredibly dangerous right now for Afghans to have something Christian on their phones. The Taliban have spies and informants everywhere." The Taliban's surveillance capability has caused Christians in Afghanistan to turn off their phones and flee to remote destinations after receiving threatening messages announcing that they will be persecuted.

The Taliban-led government's Cultural Commission issued a statement saying it aims to "eradicate ignorance of irreligion" by marrying non-Muslim girls and widows to Taliban fighters and forcing non-Muslim children to serve as soldiers. Following this announcement, Afghan Christians now fear for the safety of their children.

U.S. faith-based organizations led the representation of more than 76,000 Afghans who were evacuated to the United States between 2021 and 2022. The Canadian government also established a program to help Afghan refugees who were members of the "persecuted religious minority" and other vulnerable groups. By June 10, 2022, more than 15,000 Afghan citizens were also welcomed into Canada.

The U.S. Commission on International Religious Freedom has asked the State Department to classify the Taliban's de facto government as a "country of particular concern." In doing so, sanctions would be invoked, including, inter alia, financial and travel sanctions against Taliban officials, due to their violations of religious and individual freedoms.

The collapse of freedom.

With the collapse of cities in Afghanistan due to the Taliban resurgence, the future of the country's Christian population becomes more doubtful. The 2021 withdrawal of U.S. troops has exacerbated an already tense situation in the nation and removed another layer of stability and security from the country. Unfortunately, U.S.-backed Afghan forces have largely failed to stop the Taliban's advance. As a result, the Islamic State, Al-Qaeda and the Taliban continue to pose a massive and deadly threat to the Afghan people, with the latter controlling most of the nation.

The Christians of Afghanistan have mostly gone into hiding. There is only one Catholic chapel in the country, called the Chapel of Our Lady of Divine Providence, hidden in the Italian Embassy in Kabul and subsequently abandoned due to the 2021 Taliban offensive. The Afghan constitution severely restricts religious freedom, prohibiting the public preaching of the Christian Gospel and placing strong restrictions on conversion to Christianity.

A civil war in the already torn country is increasingly likely due to growing instability. When the Taliban take over a village, all residents are required to attend prayers at the mosque to expel any Christian converts. Whatever the structure of the Church in Afghanistan in the future, due to the resurgence of the Taliban, Afghan Christians will face a hard road.

"Men are required to grow beards, women cannot leave home without male escort and life is increasingly dangerous," the International Criminal Court warned in a report based in northern Afghanistan.

Women's rights, which have steadily improved over the years, are being rapidly curtailed, and the nearly $1 trillion invested in the 20-year duration of the conflict will bring nothing in terms of long-term development and improvement. One of the most recent changes under the Taliban regime is that student attendance at schools has been severely limited. Following the ban on female education in 2022, the Taliban decided that women can only attend university if they are segregated from male students and under a strictly imposed dress code, such as the burqa, which covers everything.

"The education and participation of women and girls in public life is fundamental to any modern society. The relegation of women and girls to the home denies Afghanistan the benefit of the important contributions they can offer. Education for all is not only a basic human right, it is the key to the progress and development of a nation," said markus Potzel, acting head of the United Nations Assistance Mission in Afghanistan.

Taliban-controlled Afghanistan is incapable of hosting any kind of religious plurality. The extinction, brutality and discrimination of religious minorities were the hallmarks of the brief Taliban administration in Afghanistan before 2001. As a result of the Taliban regime's strong enforcement of its version of Islamic sharia, all conduct deemed to be contrary to Islam was monitored and banned, and the subjugation of women reached unprecedented levels.

However, while the Taliban recently declared that they would build an "inclusive" Islamic government, it is clear that the new government is tightening its grip. Since the Taliban's record of inclusion is dismal, many human rights organizations are deeply wary of this promise of inclusion. So far, local Taliban representatives have enforced local laws on women's hair and clothing, unaccompanied women, gender segregation, instrumentsand music. Milli.

The country's U.S.-backed administration has left, and Afghan security forces have all but crumbled under the weight of their own incompetence.

Monitoring human rights developments in Afghanistan, trying to keep the Taliban at bay through multilateral engagement and protecting vulnerable people, such as Christians and other religious minorities, are key priorities for the international community.

According to Reuters, shooters invaded a Sikh temple compound in Kabul in March 2020, killing 25 people in the process. According to the statement, the Islamic State terror group claimed responsibility for the incident in a statement released after the attack; the massacre was allegedly carried out in response to India's oppression of Kashmiri Muslims.

There are indications that the Taliban are already targeting minorities. According to Amnesty International, a recent investigation found that the Taliban had killed nine ethnic Hazara men after taking control of Afghanistan's Ghazni region.

"The rights to freedom of peaceful assembly, freedom of expression and freedom of opinion are not only fundamental freedoms, but are necessary for the development and progress of a nation. They allow meaningful debate to flourish, which also benefits leaders by allowing them to better understand the issues and problems facing the population," said Fiona Frazer, head of human rights at the United Nations Assistance Mission in Afghanistan.

Christian Goals

The Taliban's victory in Afghanistan has been declared complete, and the nation's minorities, especially Afghanistan's small and hidden Christian population, live in daily terror.

Shoaib Ebadi, a partner at The Voice of the Martyrs in Canada, explained: *"Hundreds of Afghan Christians fled Afghanistan to Pakistan, Dubai and Abu Dhabi."* He went on to state that *"[believers] are under daily threat; they live in danger."*

A Christian representative, whose name was not provided for security reasons, told International Christian Concern that in the days following the collapse of Kabul, *"some well-known Christians are already receiving threatening phone calls. On these calls, unknown people say, 'We're coming for you.'"*

According to a US State Department report '2021 Report on International Religious Freedom: Afghanistan' that was published in July 2022, Mullah Booruddin Turabi, a member of the Taliban's "interim government" in September 2021, said:

"Cutting off your hands is very necessary for safety... Everyone criticized us for the punishments in the stadium, but we have never said anything about their laws and their punishments. No one will tell us what our laws should be. We will follow Islam and make our laws [based] on the Qur'an."

Turabi, who has been sanctioned in the past by the UN Security Council, also suggested carrying out these punishments in public. International non-governmental organizations fear that the country's religious minorities could be targeted.

In a statement, the field director of Open Doors Asia (who calls himself "Brother Samuel") said: *"It is a heartbreaking day for the citizens of Afghanistan and an even more dangerous time to be a Christian... Secret believers in Afghanistan are especially vulnerable."* According to the 2022 Open Door World Watch List, Afghanistan has been named the most dangerous country for Christians.

And the clock keeps ticking, ticking, ticking...

EPILOGUE

According to the end times, the fulfillment of prophecy, persecution, hatred and betrayal will be frequent.

"Then you will be given over to persecution and death, and you will be hated by all nations because of me. At that time many will turn away from the faith and betray and hate each other, and many false prophets will appear who will deceive many people. Because of the increase in evil, the love of the majority will grow cold, but the one who stands firm to the end will be saved. And this gospel of the kingdom will be preached throughout the world as a testimony to all nations, and then the end will come."
Matthew 24:9-14

According to Jesus, things will get worse and worse in the last days. However, although the apostle John predicted that many antichrists would arise, he also claimed that *"even now many antichrists have arisen"* (1 John 2:18). Christ predicted that the end would be as in the days of Noah, when every intention and imagination of the human heart was continuedand completely evil. (Read Matthew chapter 24 for a clearer picture.)

Sam Brownback, who served as the U.S. Ambassador for International Religious Freedom (2018-2021), recently explained, *"There is more Christian persecution in the world today than at any time in Christian history. And there are so many different [permutations] of Christian persecution and religious persecution."*

The Christian faith is the most persecuted religious group globally, with more than 360 million Christians suffering (or about 1 in 8) persecution worldwide. According to Open Doors USA, 100 million Christians are at risk of being interrogated, detained, tortured and killed in some countries because of their religious beliefs. *"A human rights disaster of epic proportions,"* according to theCatholic humanitarian NGO Aid to the Church in Need, is being perpetrated against believers around the world. In addition, 12 Churches or Christian institutions are being destroyed. Every day, 12 Christians are unjustly arrested or imprisoned and another five are kidnapped or abducted.

Christians around the world are subject to severe restrictions on their ability to freely practice their faith, either due to violent attacks by non-state actors or restrictive governmental legislation. As the dangers to religious freedom increase, it is critical to understand the difficulties faced by believers around the world.

According to Pew Research, there are about 2.3 Christians in the world, representing about 30% of the total population. However, Christians face the highest number of religious discriminations and are routinely persecuted by government entities or by society in 168 different countries.

Translation made with the free version of the translator www.DeepL.com/TranslatorEl March 1, Archbishop Silcano M. Tomasi C.S., permanent observer of the Holy See to the United Nations in Geneva, stated:

"Terrorist attacks againstChristians in Africa, the Middle East and Asia increased by 309% between 2003 and 2010. Approximately 70 percent of the world's population lives in countries with severe restrictions on religious beliefs and practices, and religious minorities pay the highest price."

According to researcher David B. Barrett, there have been 70 million Christian martyrs since the time of Christ. It is estimated that 45 million (65%) of them occurred in the twentieth century. In the absence of a better expression, in the last century more Christians perished for their faith than in the previous 19 centuries combined.

Christian minorities have been subjected to increasingly violent repression in a wide range of countries, from Africa and the Middle Eastto Asia and Oceania. There have been governments and their agents who have destroyed churches and imprisoned parishioners. In addition, around the world, guerrilla units and vigilantes have taken justice into their own hands, massacring Christians and driving them out of their homes.

There is no doubt that religious persecution is on the rise around the world. According to United Nations Secretary-General Antonio Guterres, *"We have seen* an increase in attacks against people targeted because of their religion or belief. The world musttake a step forward to end anti-Semitism, anti-Muslim hatred, the persecution of Christians and other religious groups. We all have a responsibility to take care of each other."

1 Pedro 4:12-19:

"Dear friends, do not be surprised at the trial by fire that has come upon you to test you, as if something strange were happening to you. On the contrary, rejoice because you participate in the sufferings of Christ, so that you may rejoice when his glory is manifested. If you areinsulted because of the name of Christ, you are blessed, for the Spirit of glory and god rests upon you. If you suffer, it should not be like a murderer or thief or any other type of criminal, or even a meddler. However, ifyou suf res as a Christian, do not be ashamed, but praise God for bearing that name. For it is time for judgment to begin with the house of God; And if it begins with us, what will be the outcome for those who do not obey the gospel of God? And if it is difficult forthe righteous to be saved, what will become of the wicked and the sinner? Thus, those who suffer according to God's will must commit themselves to their faithful Creator and continue to do good."

The countdown for Christ's return is imminent.

www.ingramcontent.com/pod-product-compliance
Lightning Source LLC
LaVergne TN
LVHW091550060526
838200LV00036B/774